GEORGE O'CONNOR

ARES
BRINGER OF WAR

A NEAL PORTER BOOK

First Second

New York

TO KNOW THE GREAT GOD ARES,
YOU MUST FIRST KNOW HOW HE
DIFFERS FROM ATHENA.

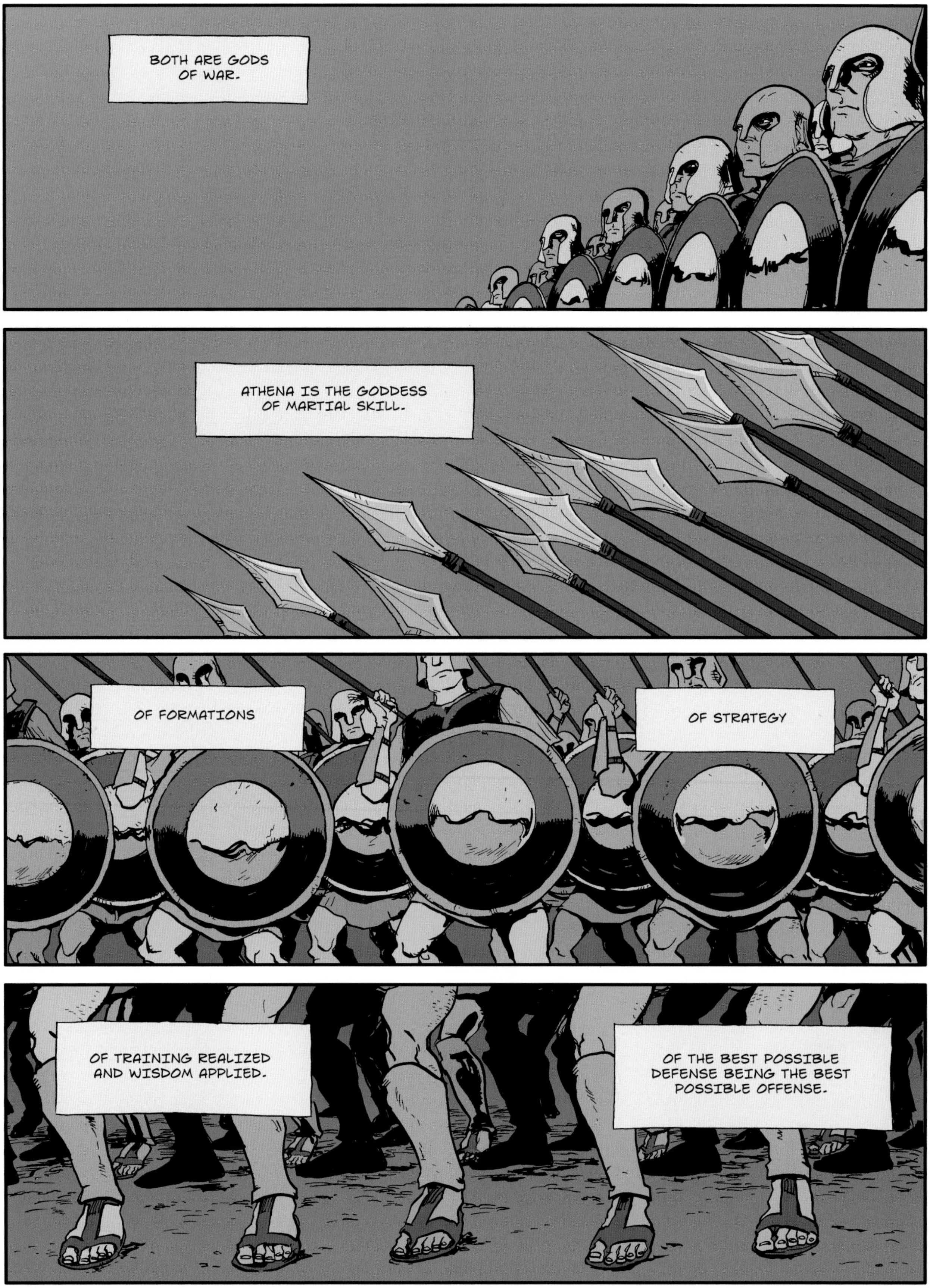
BOTH ARE GODS OF WAR.
ATHENA IS THE GODDESS OF MARTIAL SKILL.
OF FORMATIONS
OF STRATEGY
OF TRAINING REALIZED AND WISDOM APPLIED.
OF THE BEST POSSIBLE DEFENSE BEING THE BEST POSSIBLE OFFENSE.

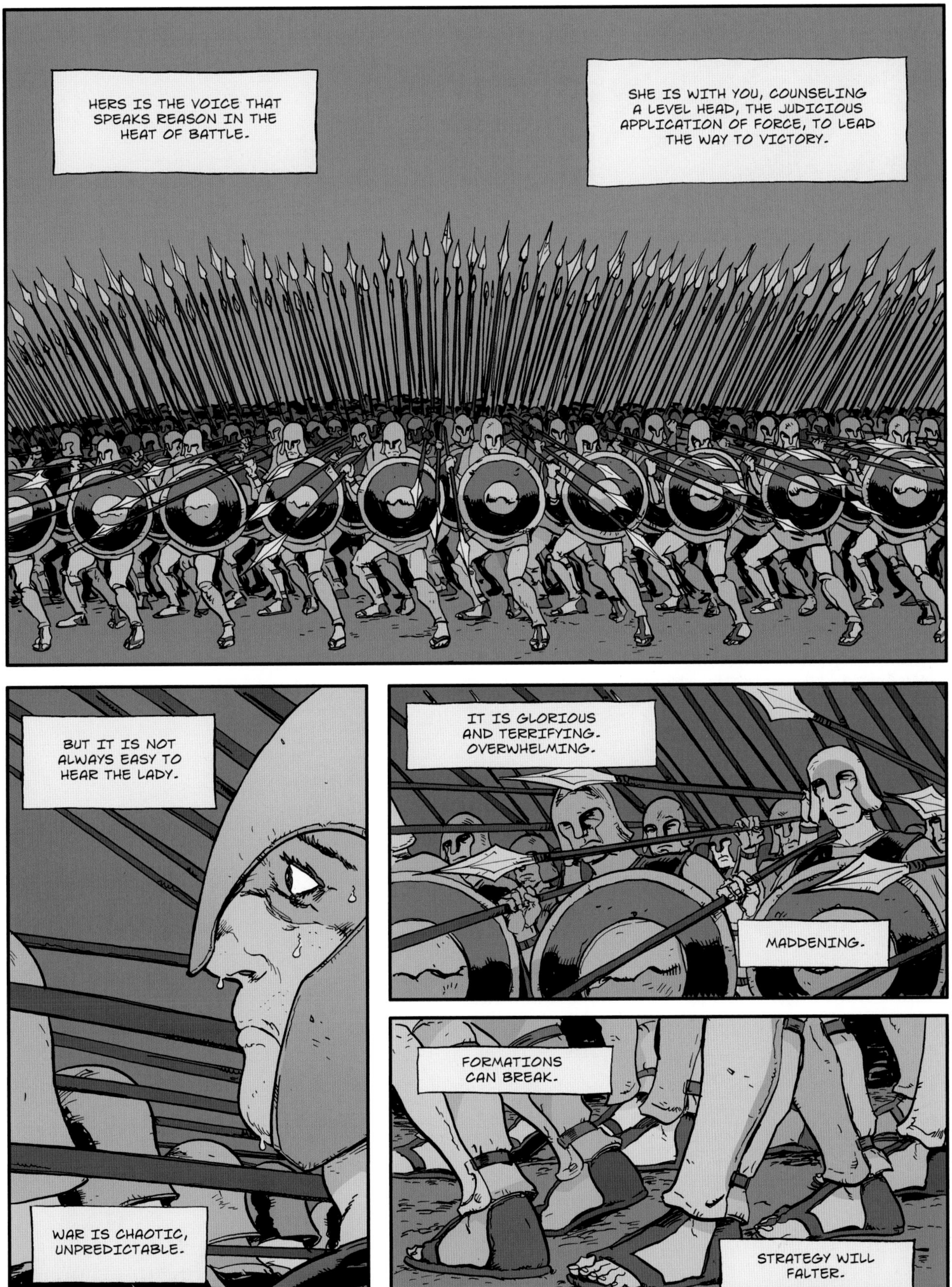
HERS IS THE VOICE THAT SPEAKS REASON IN THE HEAT OF BATTLE.
SHE IS WITH YOU, COUNSELING A LEVEL HEAD, THE JUDICIOUS APPLICATION OF FORCE, TO LEAD THE WAY TO VICTORY.
BUT IT IS NOT ALWAYS EASY TO HEAR THE LADY.
WAR IS CHAOTIC, UNPREDICTABLE.
IT IS GLORIOUS AND TERRIFYING. OVERWHELMING.
MADDENING.
FORMATIONS CAN BREAK.
STRATEGY WILL FALTER.

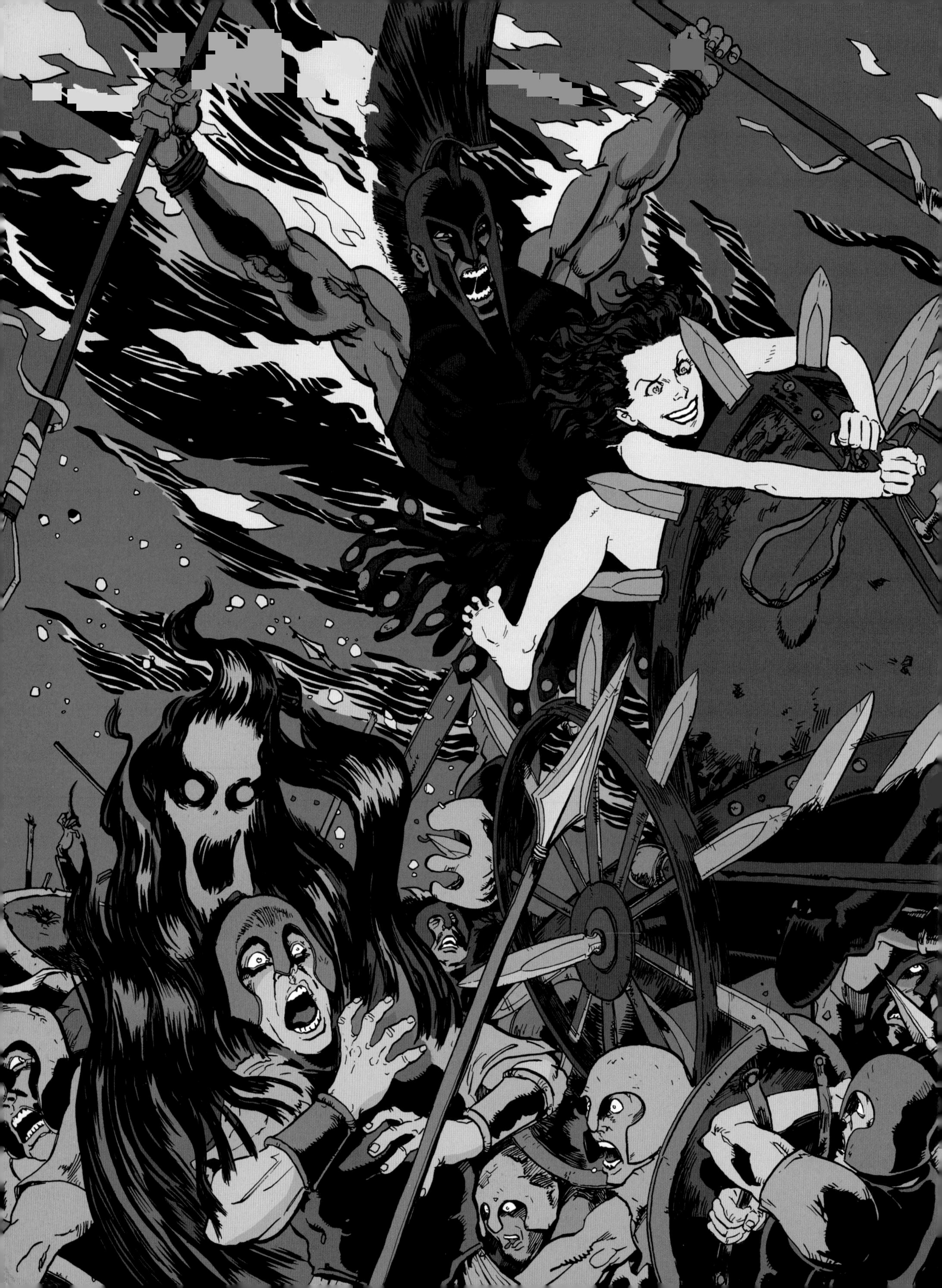

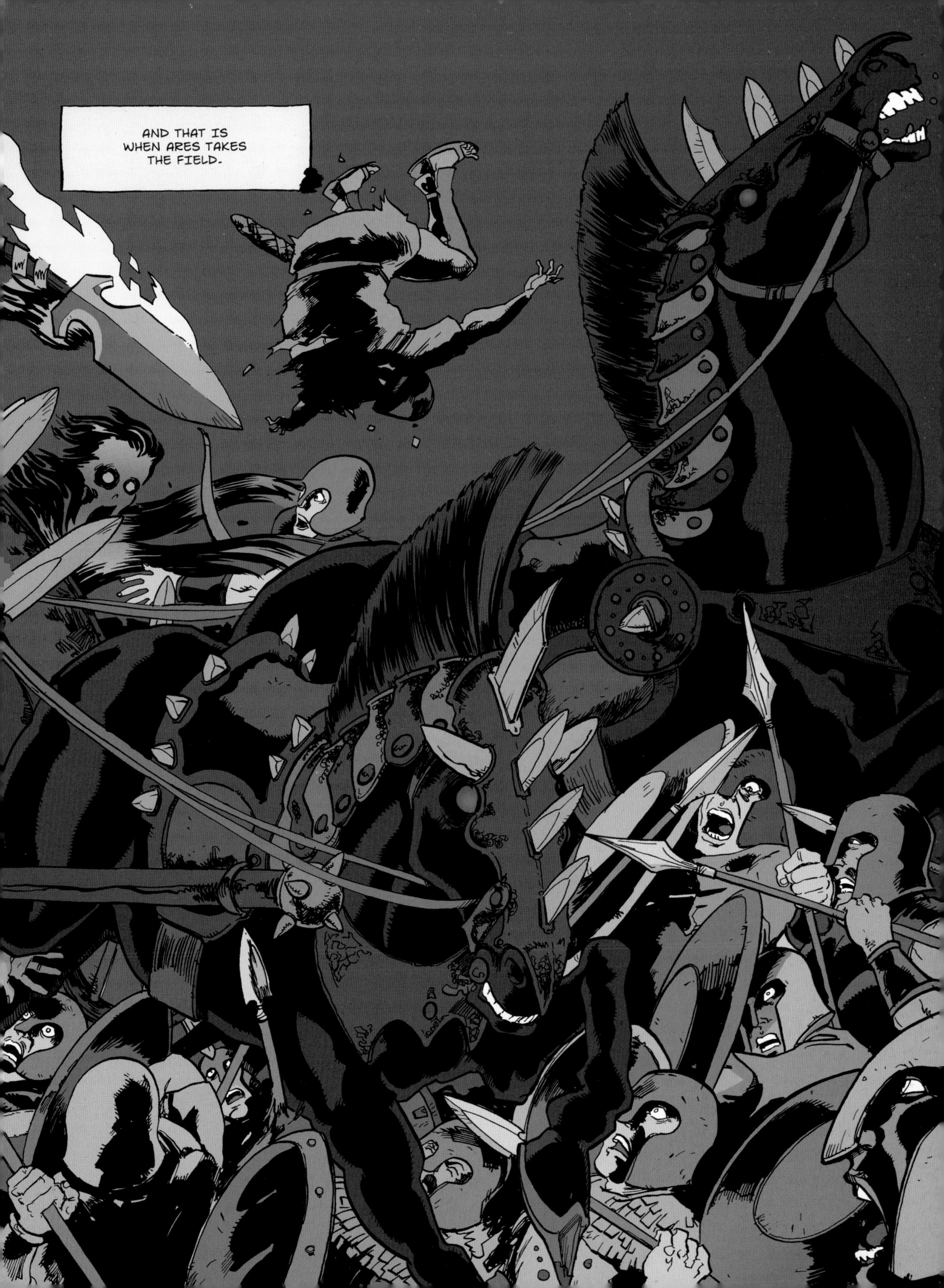
AND THAT IS
WHEN ARES TAKES
THE FIELD.

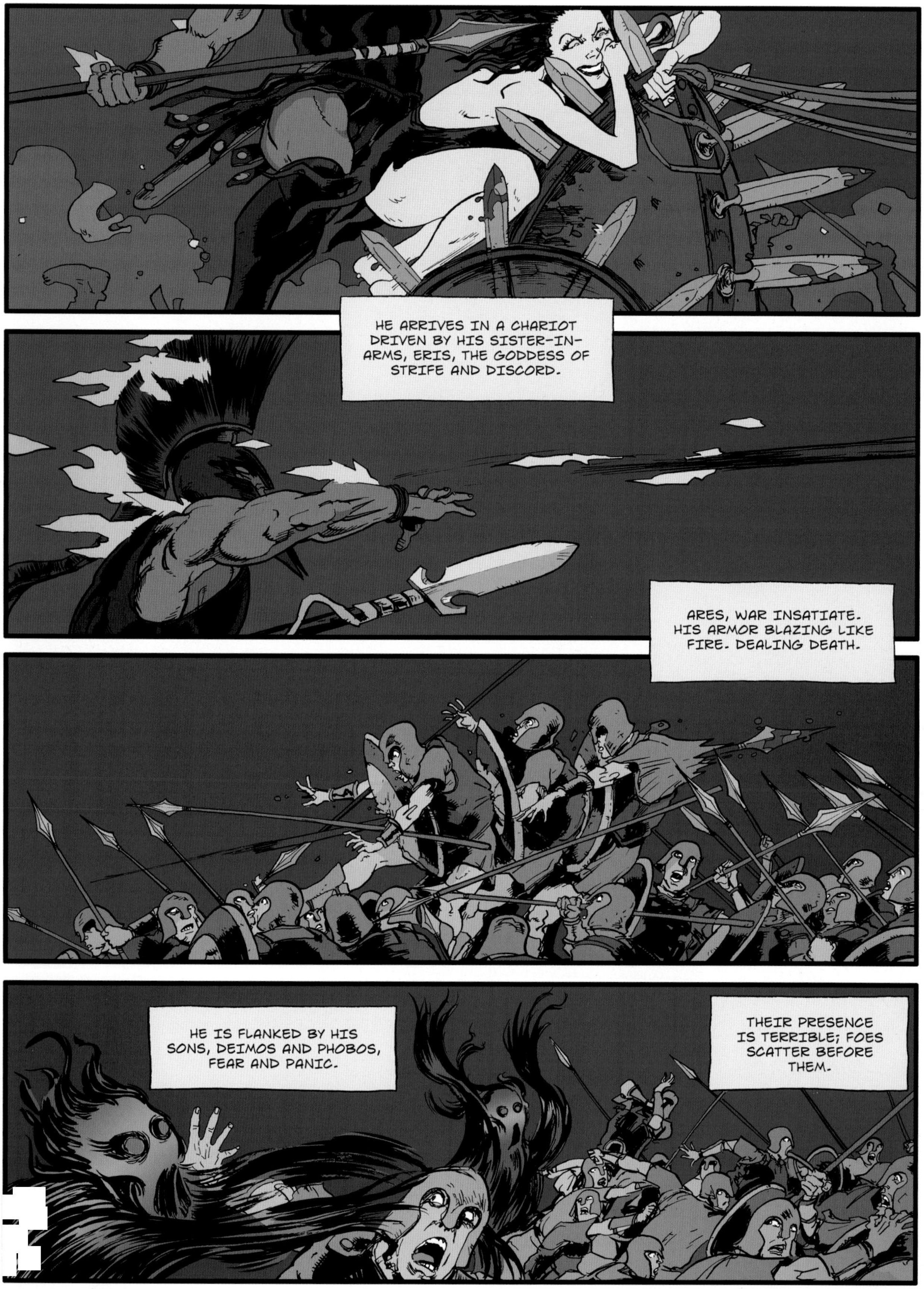
HE ARRIVES IN A CHARIOT DRIVEN BY HIS SISTER-IN-ARMS, ERIS, THE GODDESS OF STRIFE AND DISCORD.
ARES, WAR INSATIATE. HIS ARMOR BLAZING LIKE FIRE. DEALING DEATH.
HE IS FLANKED BY HIS SONS, DEIMOS AND PHOBOS, FEAR AND PANIC.
THEIR PRESENCE IS TERRIBLE; FOES SCATTER BEFORE THEM.

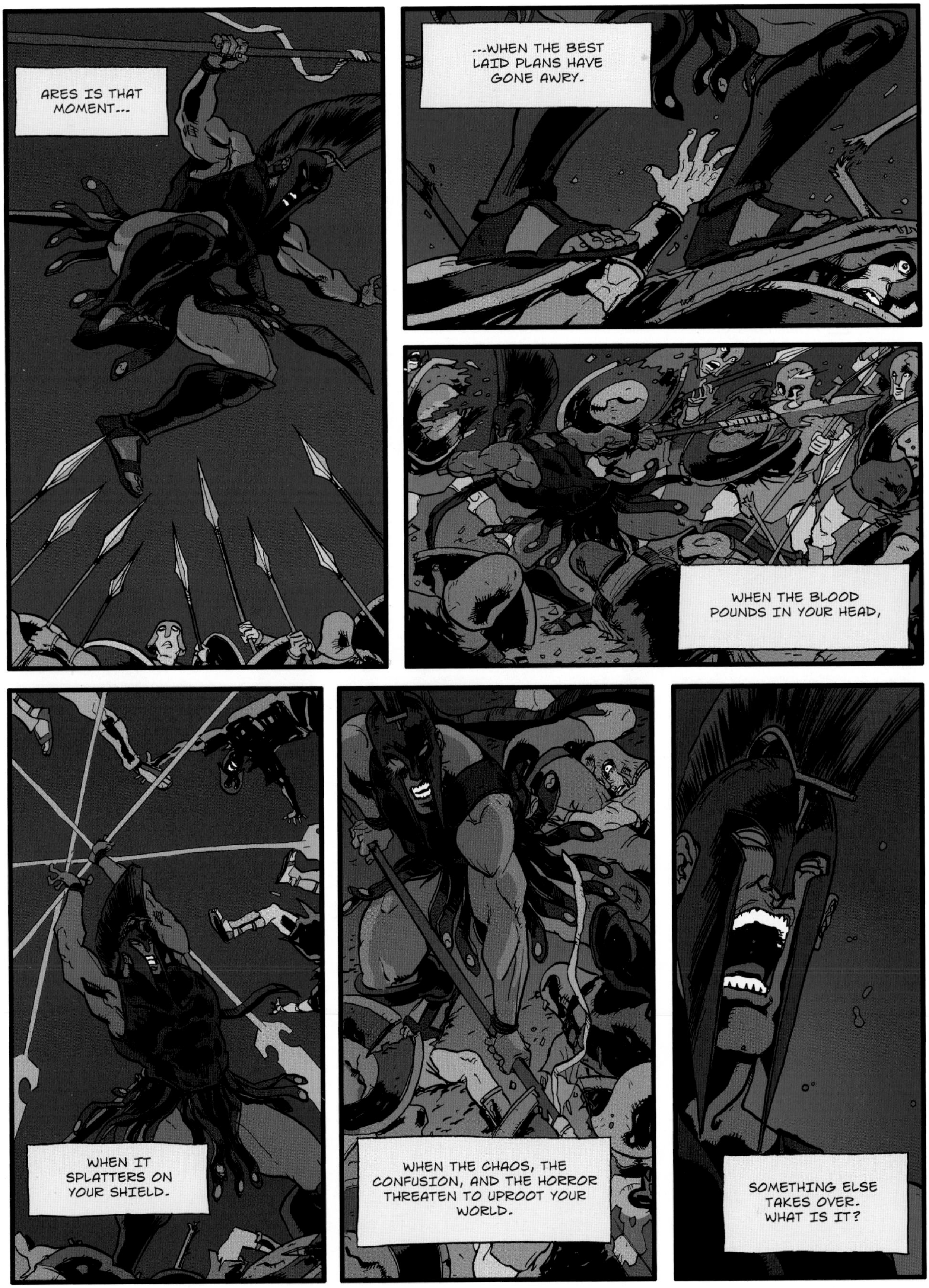
ARES IS THAT MOMENT...
...WHEN THE BEST LAID PLANS HAVE GONE AWRY.
WHEN THE BLOOD POUNDS IN YOUR HEAD,
WHEN IT SPLATTERS ON YOUR SHIELD.
WHEN THE CHAOS, THE CONFUSION, AND THE HORROR THREATEN TO UPROOT YOUR WORLD.
SOMETHING ELSE TAKES OVER. WHAT IS IT?

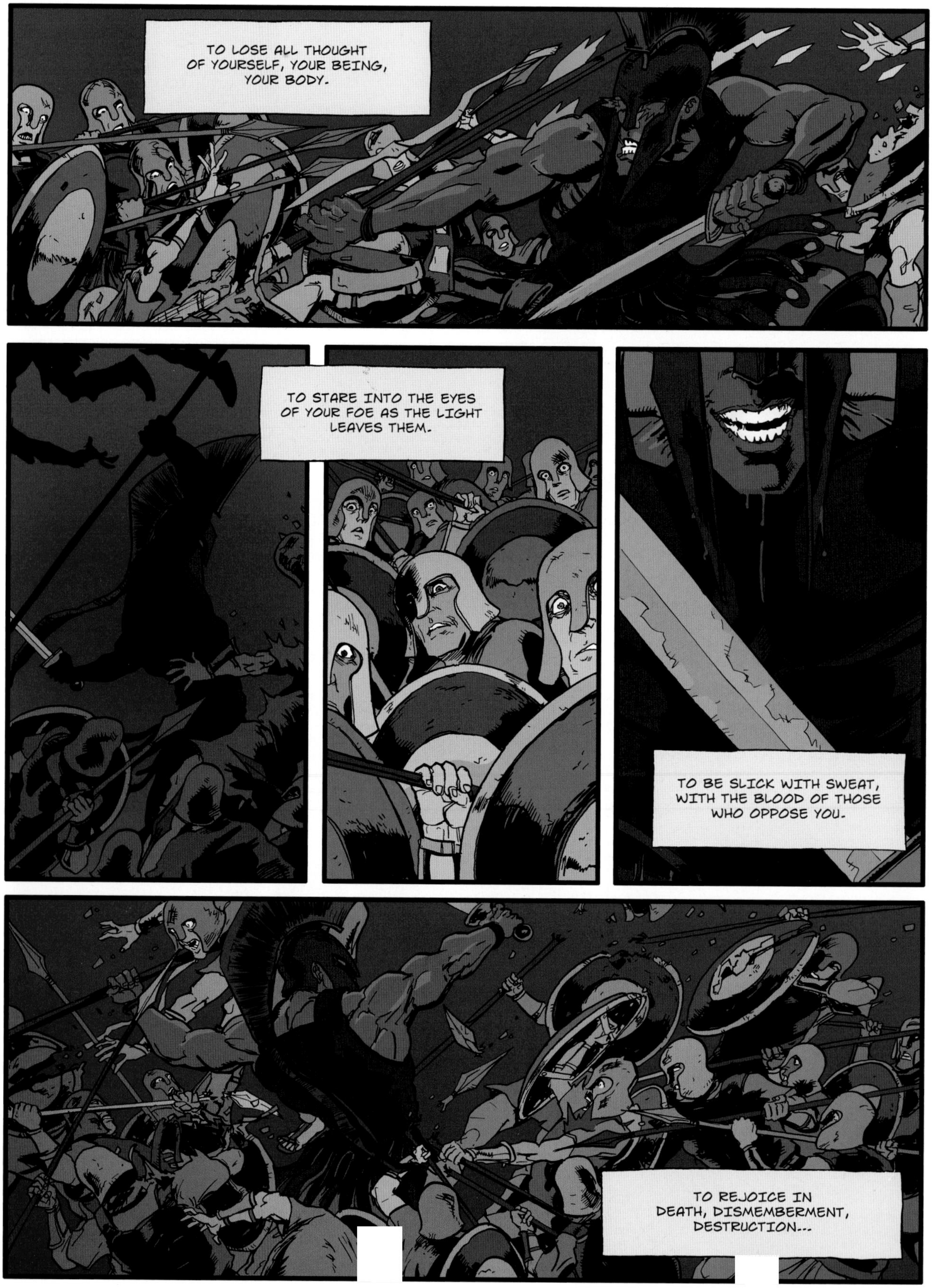

TO LOSE ALL THOUGHT OF YOURSELF, YOUR BEING, YOUR BODY.
TO STARE INTO THE EYES OF YOUR FOE AS THE LIGHT LEAVES THEM.
TO BE SLICK WITH SWEAT, WITH THE BLOOD OF THOSE WHO OPPOSE YOU.
TO REJOICE IN DEATH, DISMEMBERMENT, DESTRUCTION...

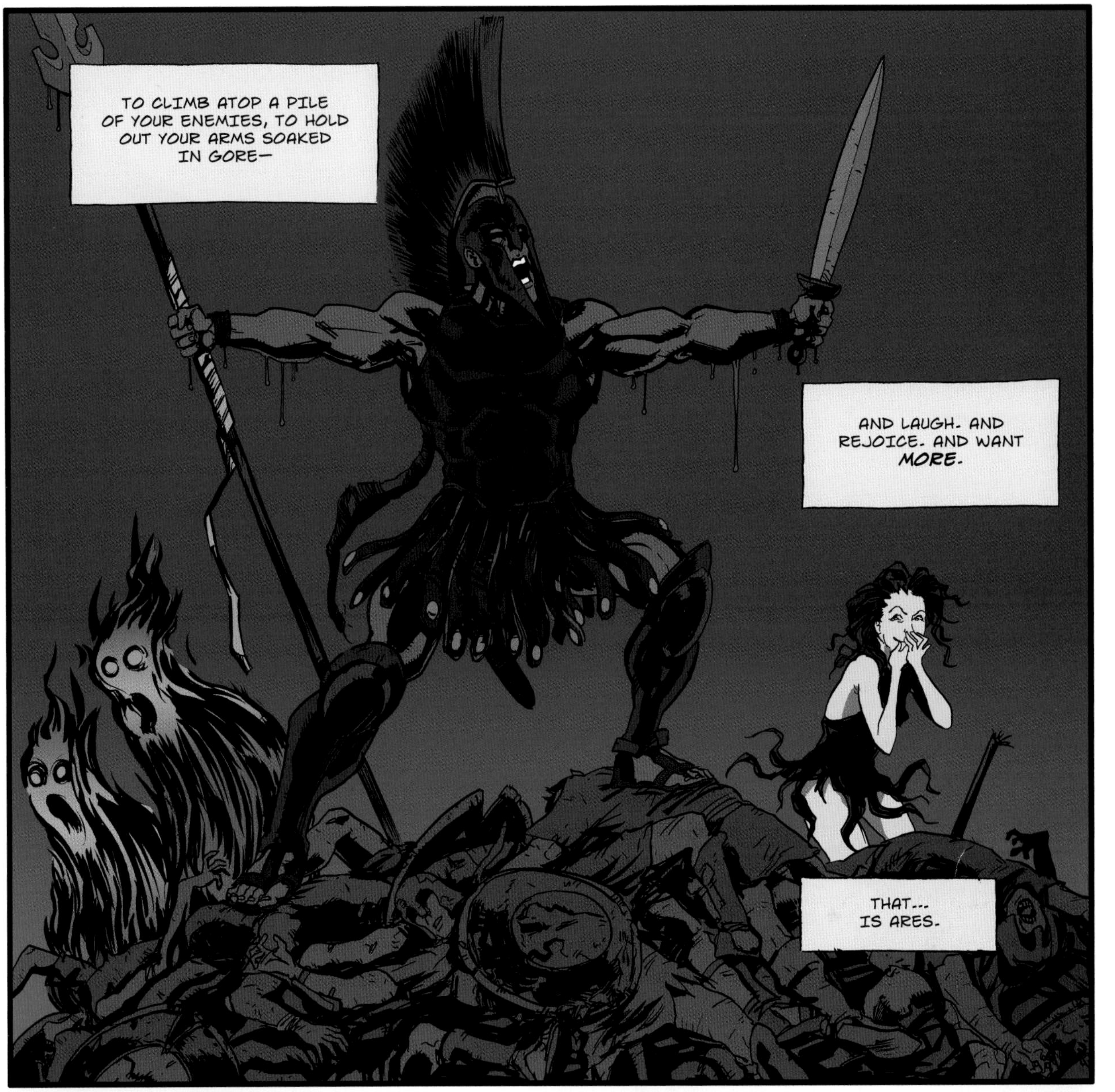
TO CLIMB ATOP A PILE OF YOUR ENEMIES, TO HOLD OUT YOUR ARMS SOAKED IN GORE—
AND LAUGH. AND REJOICE. AND WANT *MORE*.
THAT... IS ARES.

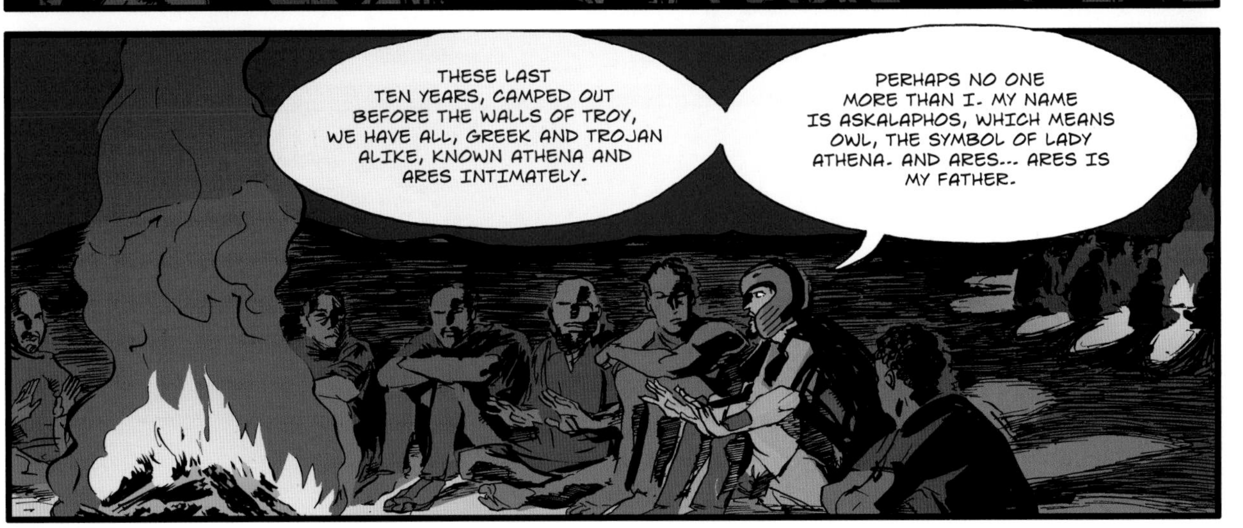
THESE LAST TEN YEARS, CAMPED OUT BEFORE THE WALLS OF TROY, WE HAVE ALL, GREEK AND TROJAN ALIKE, KNOWN ATHENA AND ARES INTIMATELY.
PERHAPS NO ONE MORE THAN I. MY NAME IS ASKALAPHOS, WHICH MEANS OWL, THE SYMBOL OF LADY ATHENA. AND ARES... ARES IS MY FATHER.

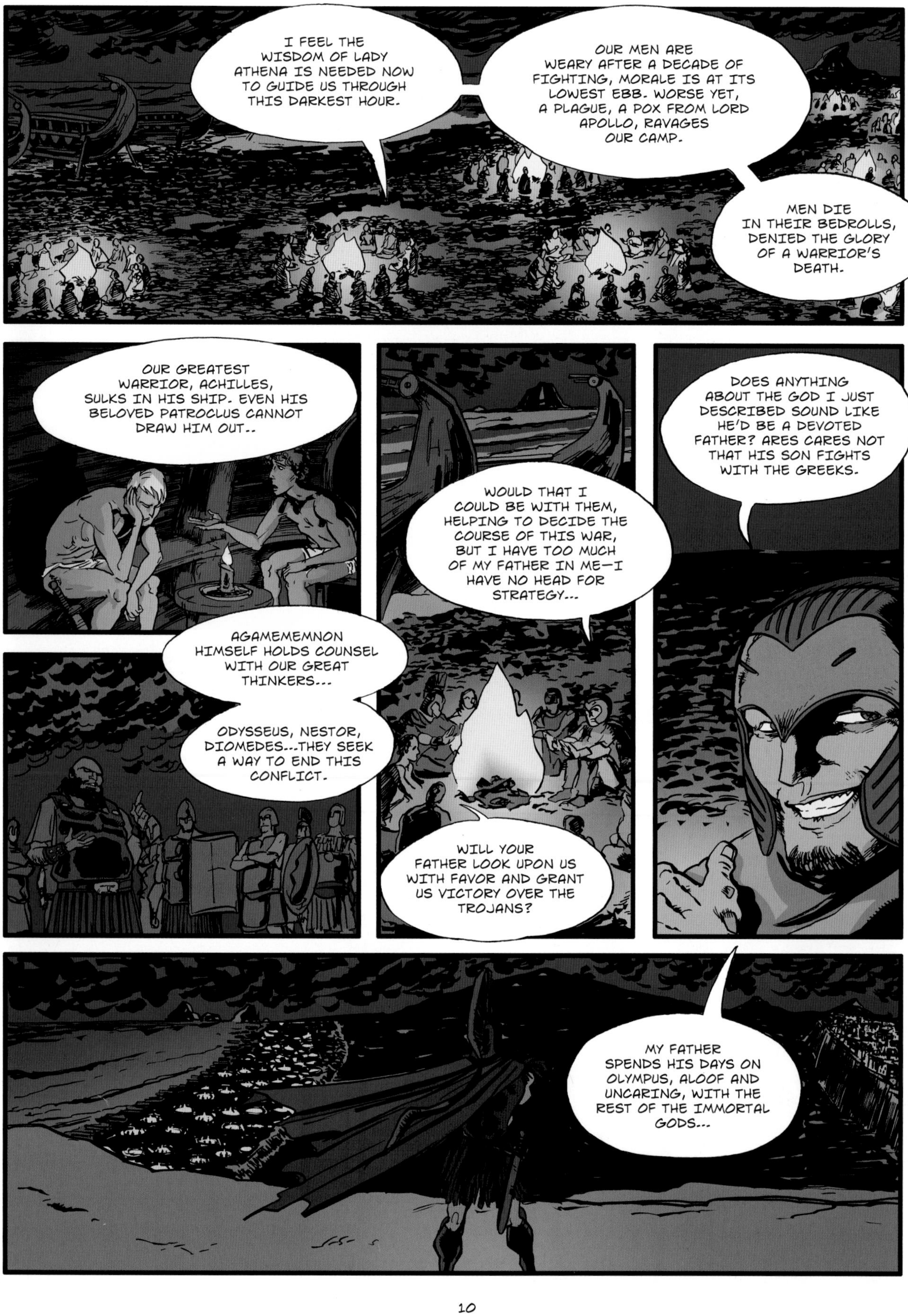
I FEEL THE WISDOM OF LADY ATHENA IS NEEDED NOW TO GUIDE US THROUGH THIS DARKEST HOUR.
OUR MEN ARE WEARY AFTER A DECADE OF FIGHTING, MORALE IS AT ITS LOWEST EBB. WORSE YET, A PLAGUE, A POX FROM LORD APOLLO, RAVAGES OUR CAMP.
MEN DIE IN THEIR BEDROLLS, DENIED THE GLORY OF A WARRIOR'S DEATH.
OUR GREATEST WARRIOR, ACHILLES, SULKS IN HIS SHIP. EVEN HIS BELOVED PATROCLUS CANNOT DRAW HIM OUT..
AGAMEMEMNON HIMSELF HOLDS COUNSEL WITH OUR GREAT THINKERS...
ODYSSEUS, NESTOR, DIOMEDES...THEY SEEK A WAY TO END THIS CONFLICT.
WOULD THAT I COULD BE WITH THEM, HELPING TO DECIDE THE COURSE OF THIS WAR, BUT I HAVE TOO MUCH OF MY FATHER IN ME—I HAVE NO HEAD FOR STRATEGY...
WILL YOUR FATHER LOOK UPON US WITH FAVOR AND GRANT US VICTORY OVER THE TROJANS?
DOES ANYTHING ABOUT THE GOD I JUST DESCRIBED SOUND LIKE HE'D BE A DEVOTED FATHER? ARES CARES NOT THAT HIS SON FIGHTS WITH THE GREEKS.
MY FATHER SPENDS HIS DAYS ON OLYMPUS, ALOOF AND UNCARING, WITH THE REST OF THE IMMORTAL GODS...

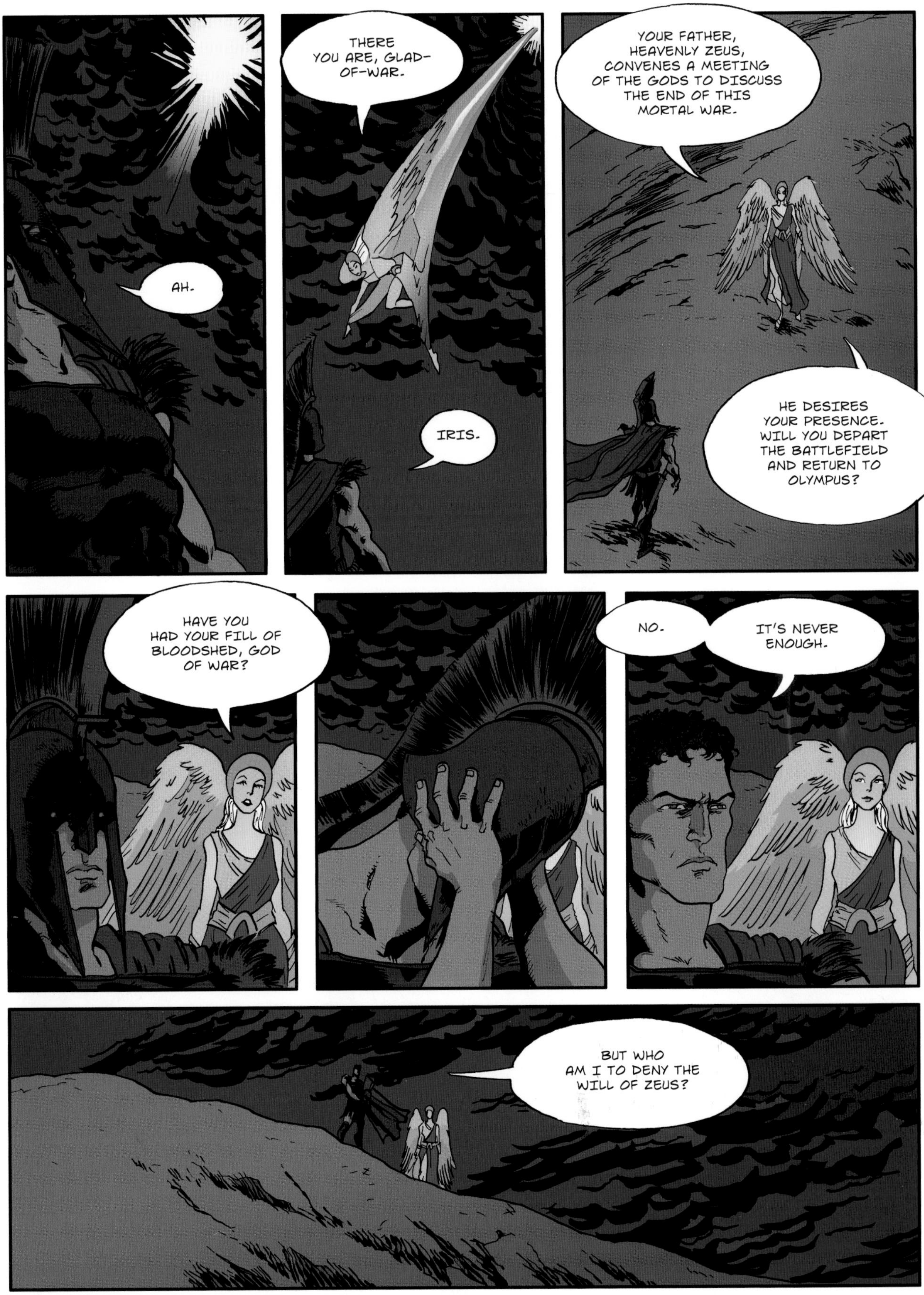
AH.
THERE YOU ARE, GLAD-OF-WAR.
IRIS.
YOUR FATHER, HEAVENLY ZEUS, CONVENES A MEETING OF THE GODS TO DISCUSS THE END OF THIS MORTAL WAR.
HE DESIRES YOUR PRESENCE. WILL YOU DEPART THE BATTLEFIELD AND RETURN TO OLYMPUS?
HAVE YOU HAD YOUR FILL OF BLOODSHED, GOD OF WAR?
NO.
IT'S NEVER ENOUGH.
BUT WHO AM I TO DENY THE WILL OF ZEUS?

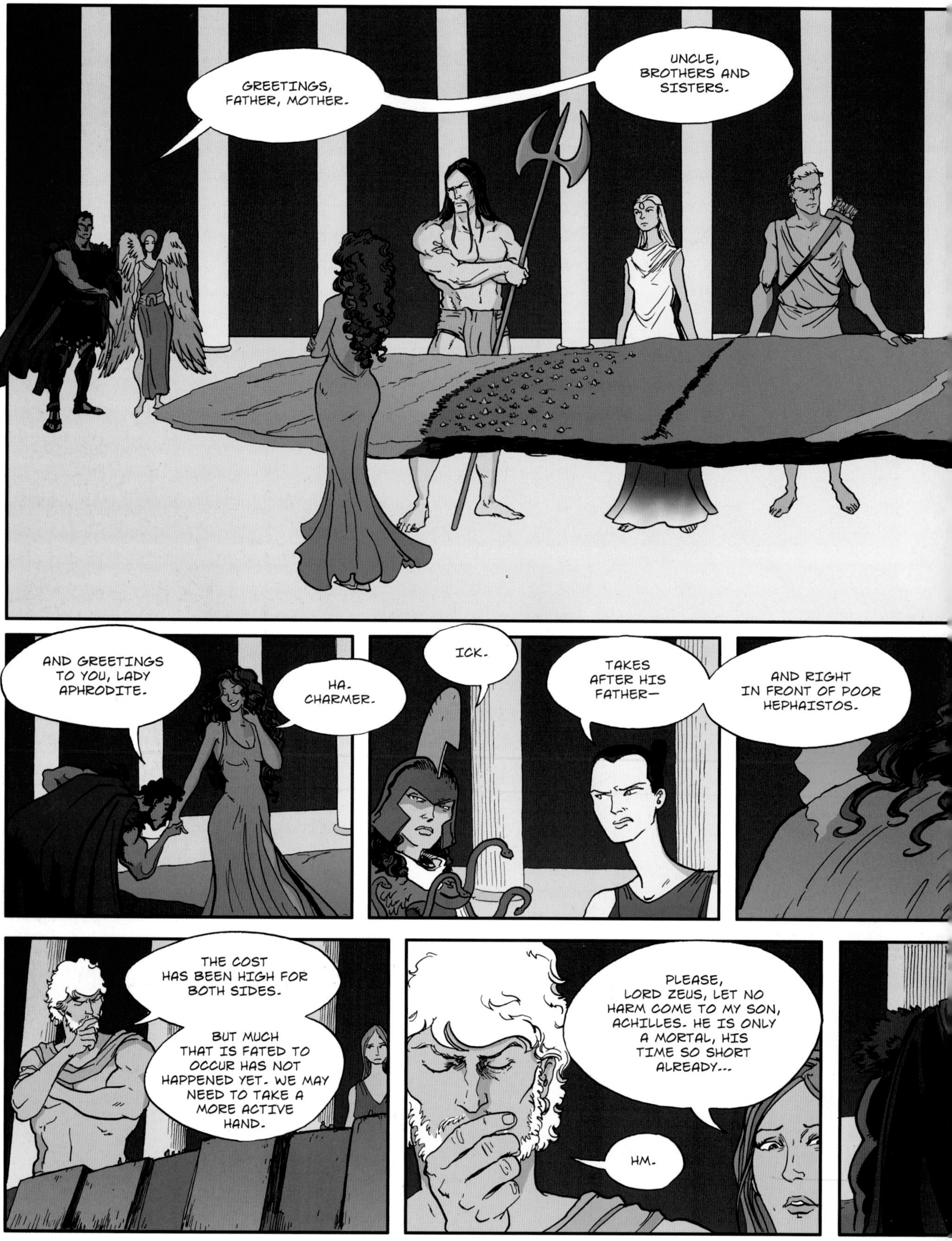
GREETINGS, FATHER, MOTHER.
UNCLE, BROTHERS AND SISTERS.
AND GREETINGS TO YOU, LADY APHRODITE.
HA. CHARMER.
ICK.
TAKES AFTER HIS FATHER—
AND RIGHT IN FRONT OF POOR HEPHAISTOS.
THE COST HAS BEEN HIGH FOR BOTH SIDES.
BUT MUCH THAT IS FATED TO OCCUR HAS NOT HAPPENED YET. WE MAY NEED TO TAKE A MORE ACTIVE HAND.
PLEASE, LORD ZEUS, LET NO HARM COME TO MY SON, ACHILLES. HE IS ONLY A MORTAL, HIS TIME SO SHORT ALREADY...
HM.

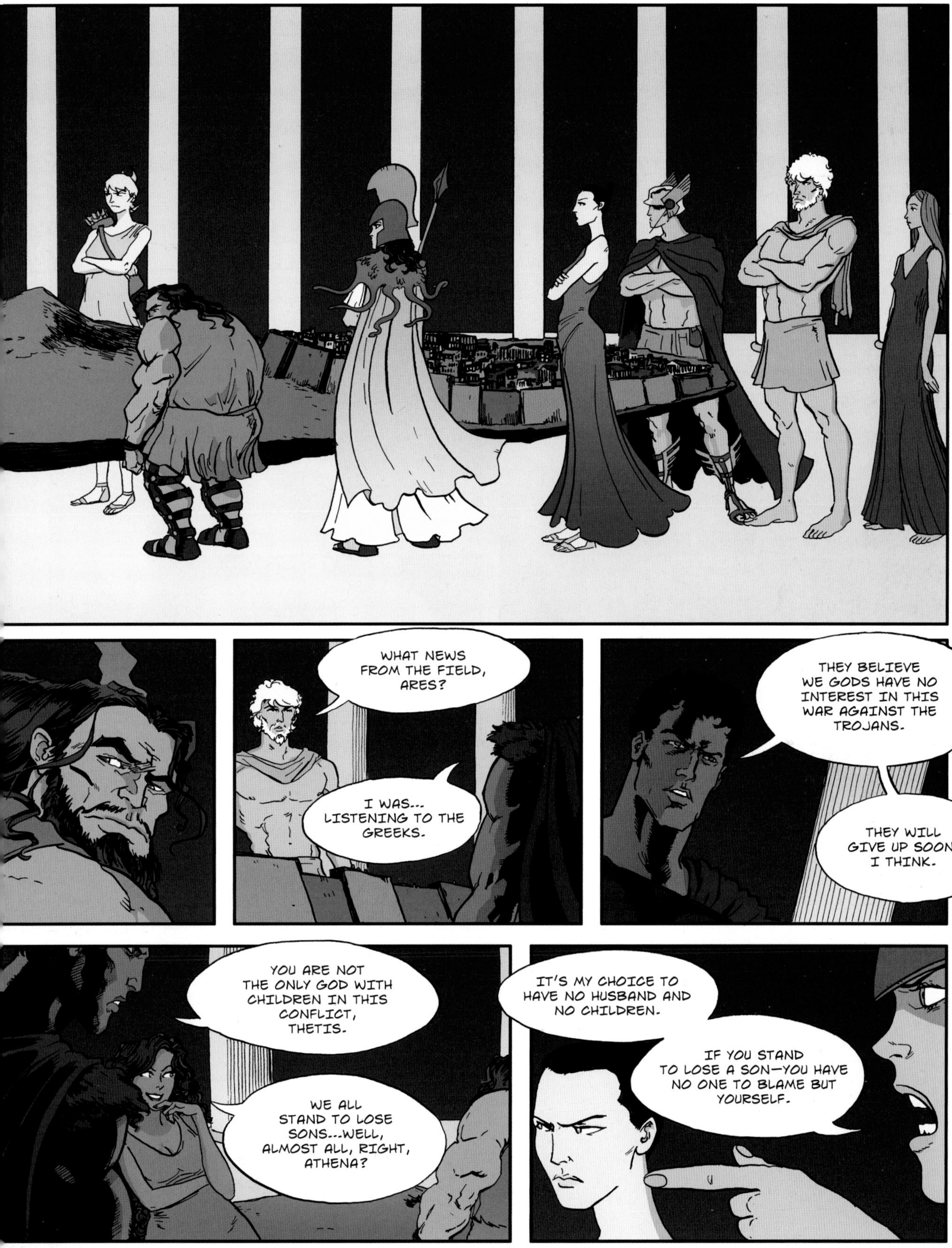
WHAT NEWS FROM THE FIELD, ARES?
I WAS... LISTENING TO THE GREEKS.
THEY BELIEVE WE GODS HAVE NO INTEREST IN THIS WAR AGAINST THE TROJANS.
THEY WILL GIVE UP SOON, I THINK.
YOU ARE NOT THE ONLY GOD WITH CHILDREN IN THIS CONFLICT, THETIS.
WE ALL STAND TO LOSE SONS...WELL, ALMOST ALL, RIGHT, ATHENA?
IT'S MY CHOICE TO HAVE NO HUSBAND AND NO CHILDREN.
IF YOU STAND TO LOSE A SON—YOU HAVE NO ONE TO BLAME BUT YOURSELF.

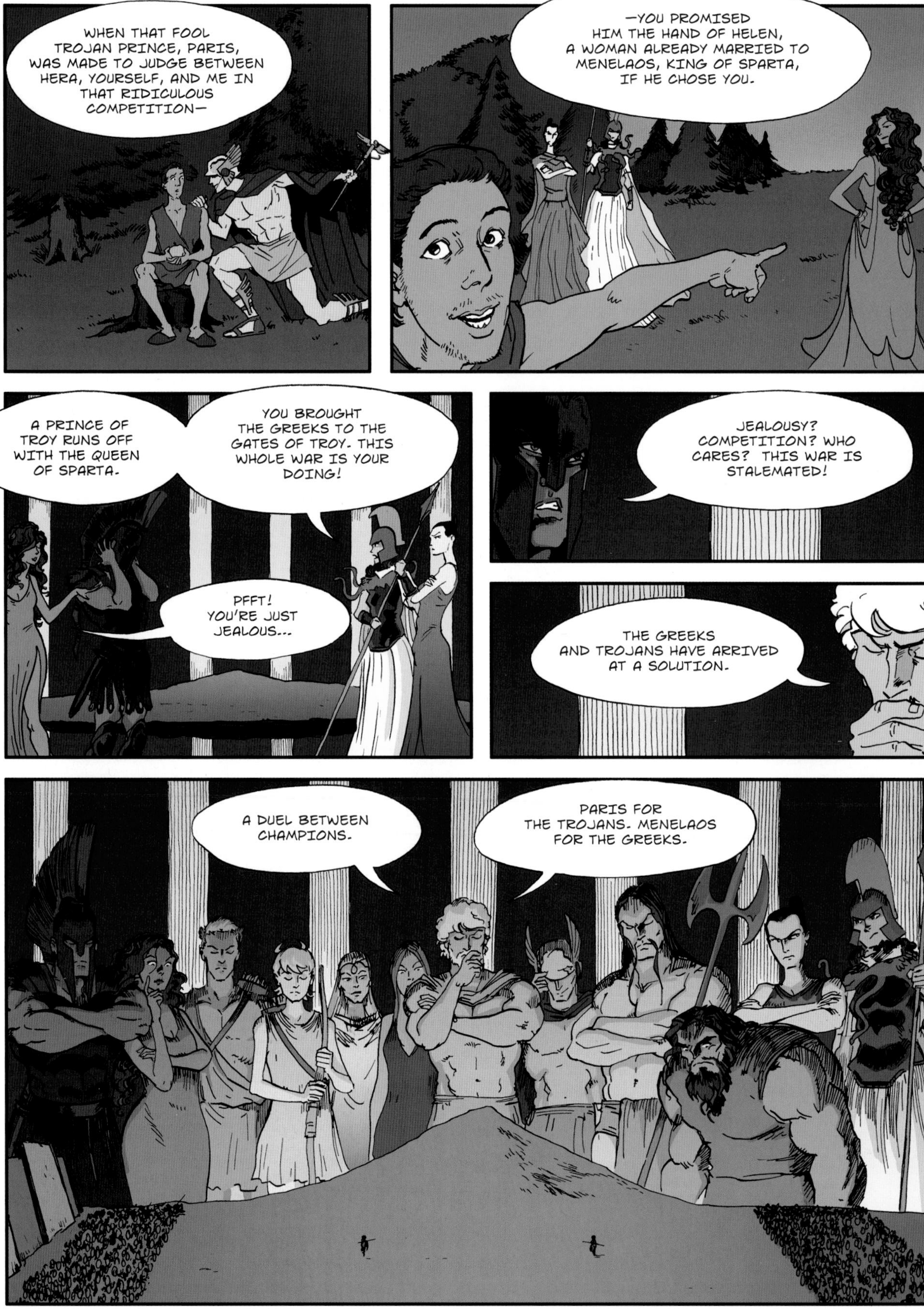

WHEN THAT FOOL TROJAN PRINCE, PARIS, WAS MADE TO JUDGE BETWEEN HERA, YOURSELF, AND ME IN THAT RIDICULOUS COMPETITION—
—YOU PROMISED HIM THE HAND OF HELEN, A WOMAN ALREADY MARRIED TO MENELAOS, KING OF SPARTA, IF HE CHOSE YOU.
A PRINCE OF TROY RUNS OFF WITH THE QUEEN OF SPARTA.
YOU BROUGHT THE GREEKS TO THE GATES OF TROY. THIS WHOLE WAR IS YOUR DOING!
PFFT! YOU'RE JUST JEALOUS...
JEALOUSY? COMPETITION? WHO CARES? THIS WAR IS STALEMATED!
THE GREEKS AND TROJANS HAVE ARRIVED AT A SOLUTION.
A DUEL BETWEEN CHAMPIONS.
PARIS FOR THE TROJANS. MENELAOS FOR THE GREEKS.

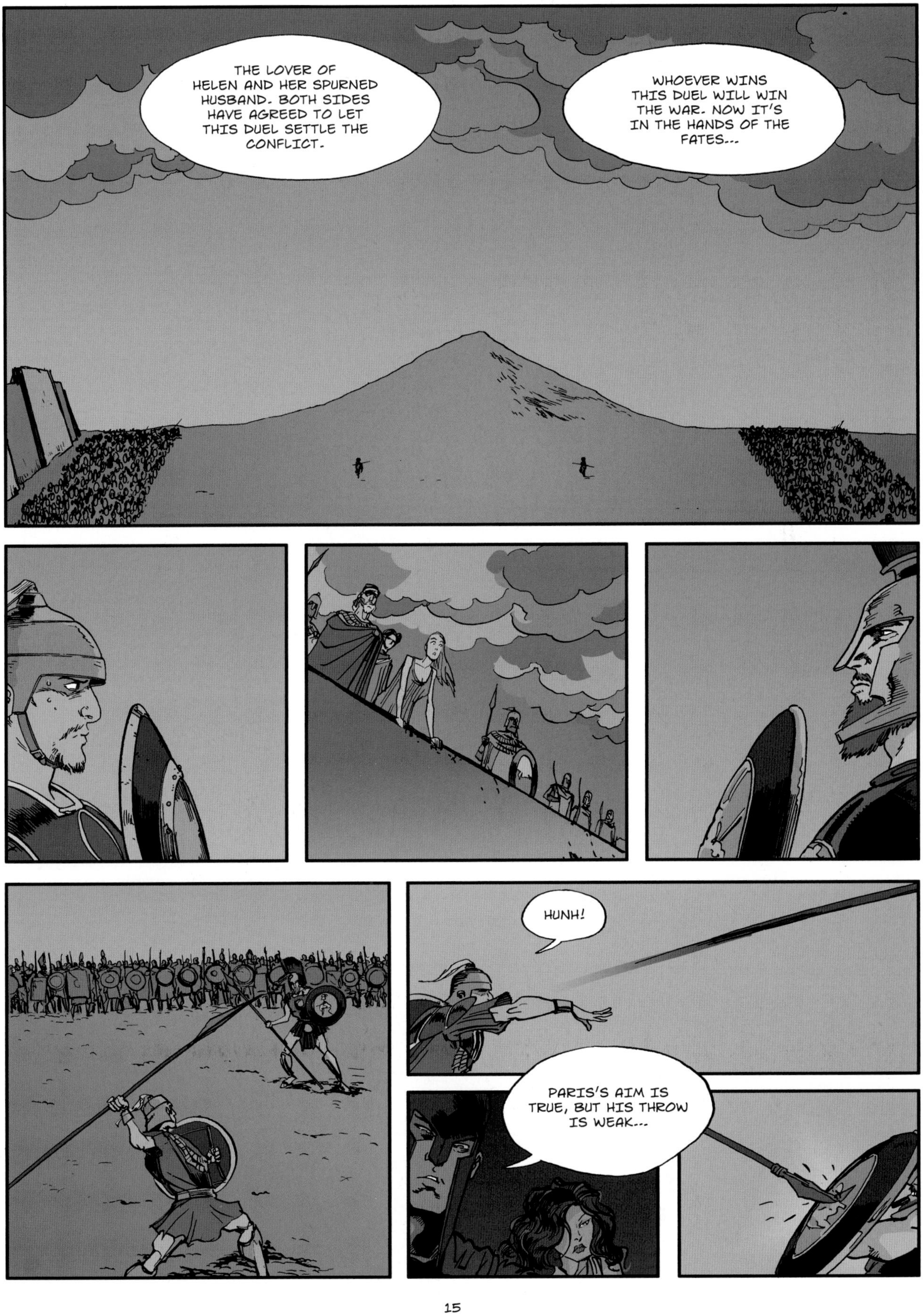
THE LOVER OF HELEN AND HER SPURNED HUSBAND. BOTH SIDES HAVE AGREED TO LET THIS DUEL SETTLE THE CONFLICT.
WHOEVER WINS THIS DUEL WILL WIN THE WAR. NOW IT'S IN THE HANDS OF THE FATES...
HUNH!
PARIS'S AIM IS TRUE, BUT HIS THROW IS WEAK...

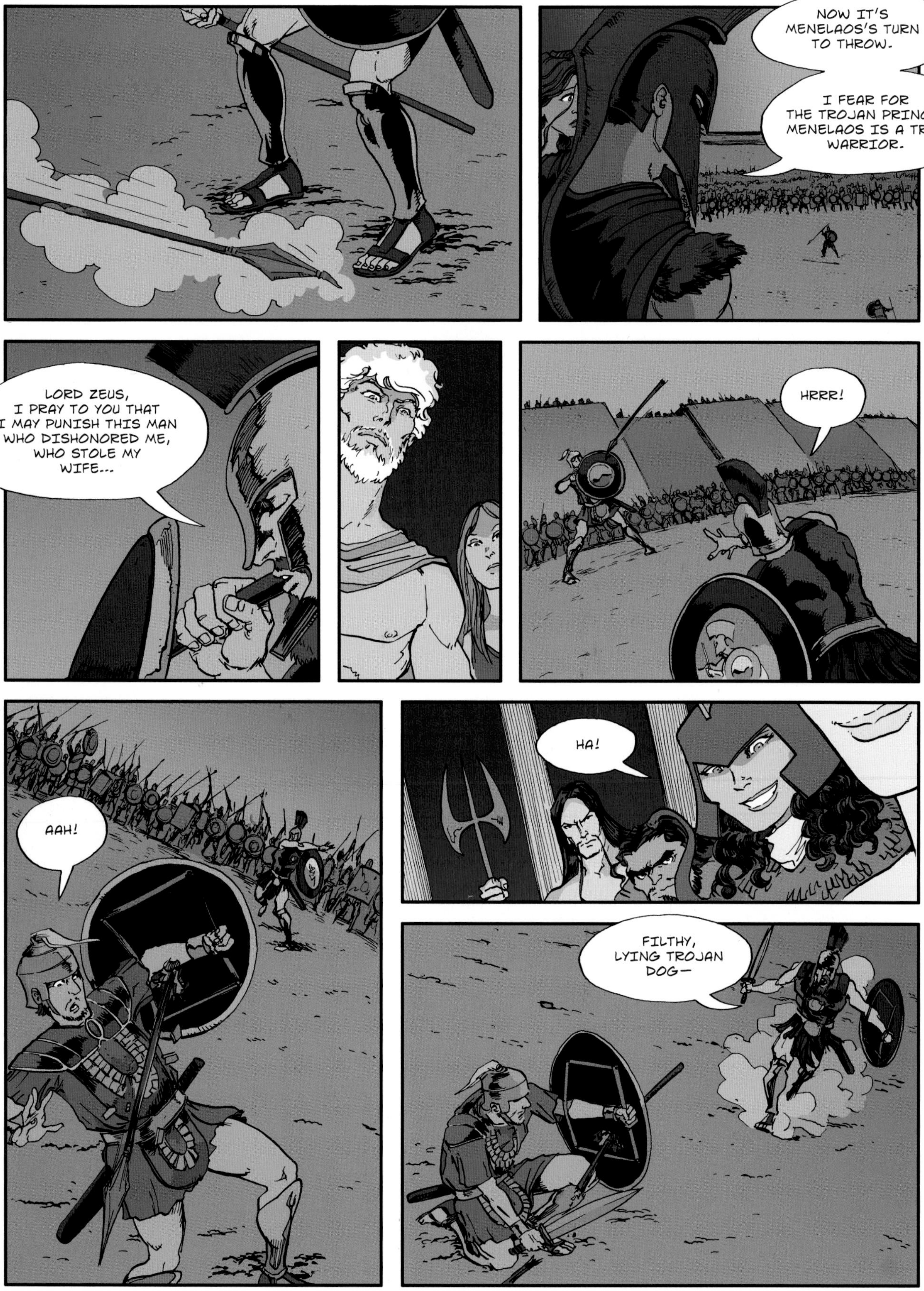
NOW IT'S MENELAOS'S TURN TO THROW.
I FEAR FOR THE TROJAN PRINCE. MENELAOS IS A TRUE WARRIOR.
LORD ZEUS, I PRAY TO YOU THAT I MAY PUNISH THIS MAN WHO DISHONORED ME, WHO STOLE MY WIFE...
HRRR!
AAH!
HA!
FILTHY, LYING TROJAN DOG—

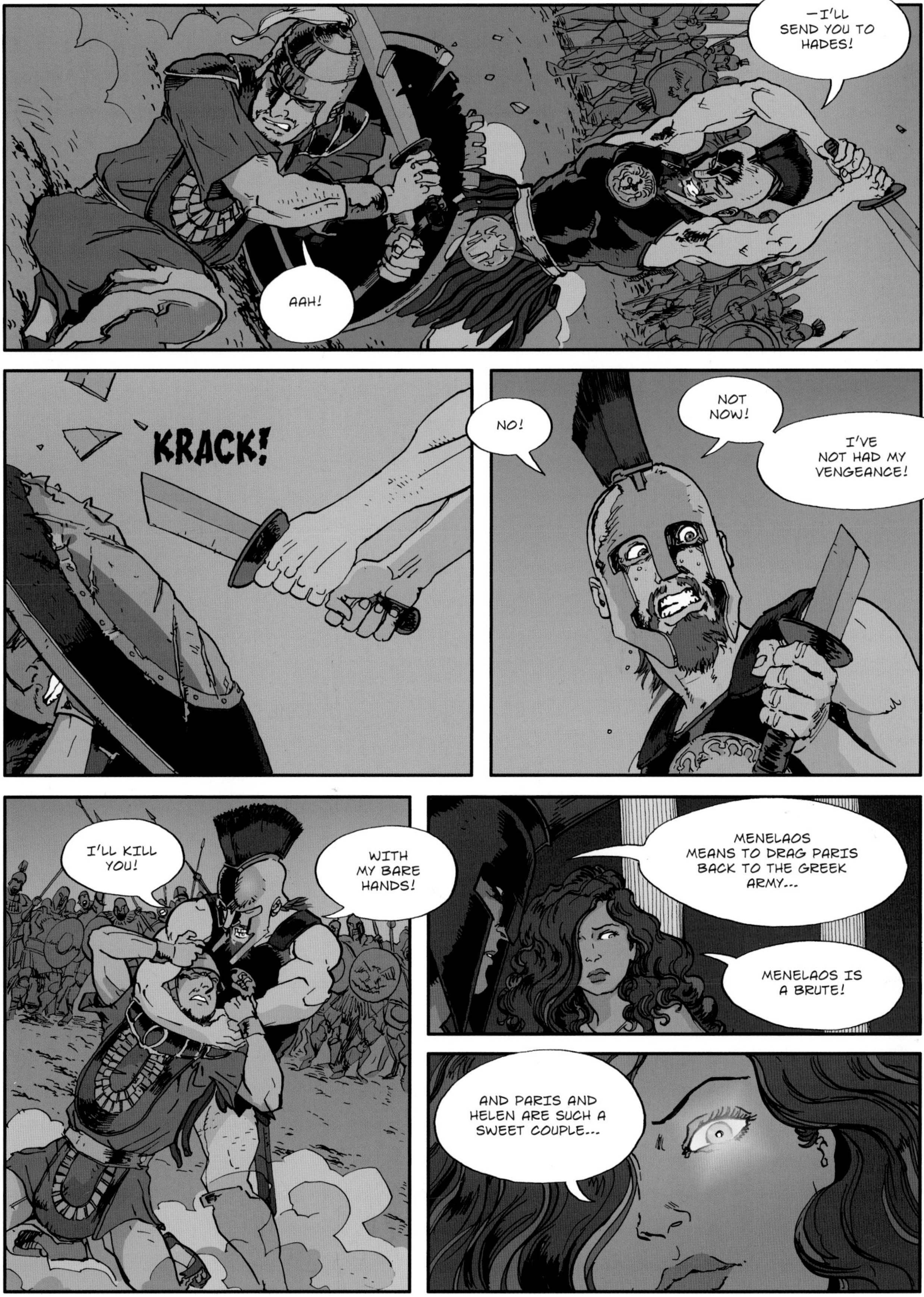

—I'LL SEND YOU TO HADES!
AAH!
KRACK!
NO!
NOT NOW!
I'VE NOT HAD MY VENGEANCE!
I'LL KILL YOU!
WITH MY BARE HANDS!
MENELAOS MEANS TO DRAG PARIS BACK TO THE GREEK ARMY...
MENELAOS IS A BRUTE!
AND PARIS AND HELEN ARE SUCH A SWEET COUPLE...

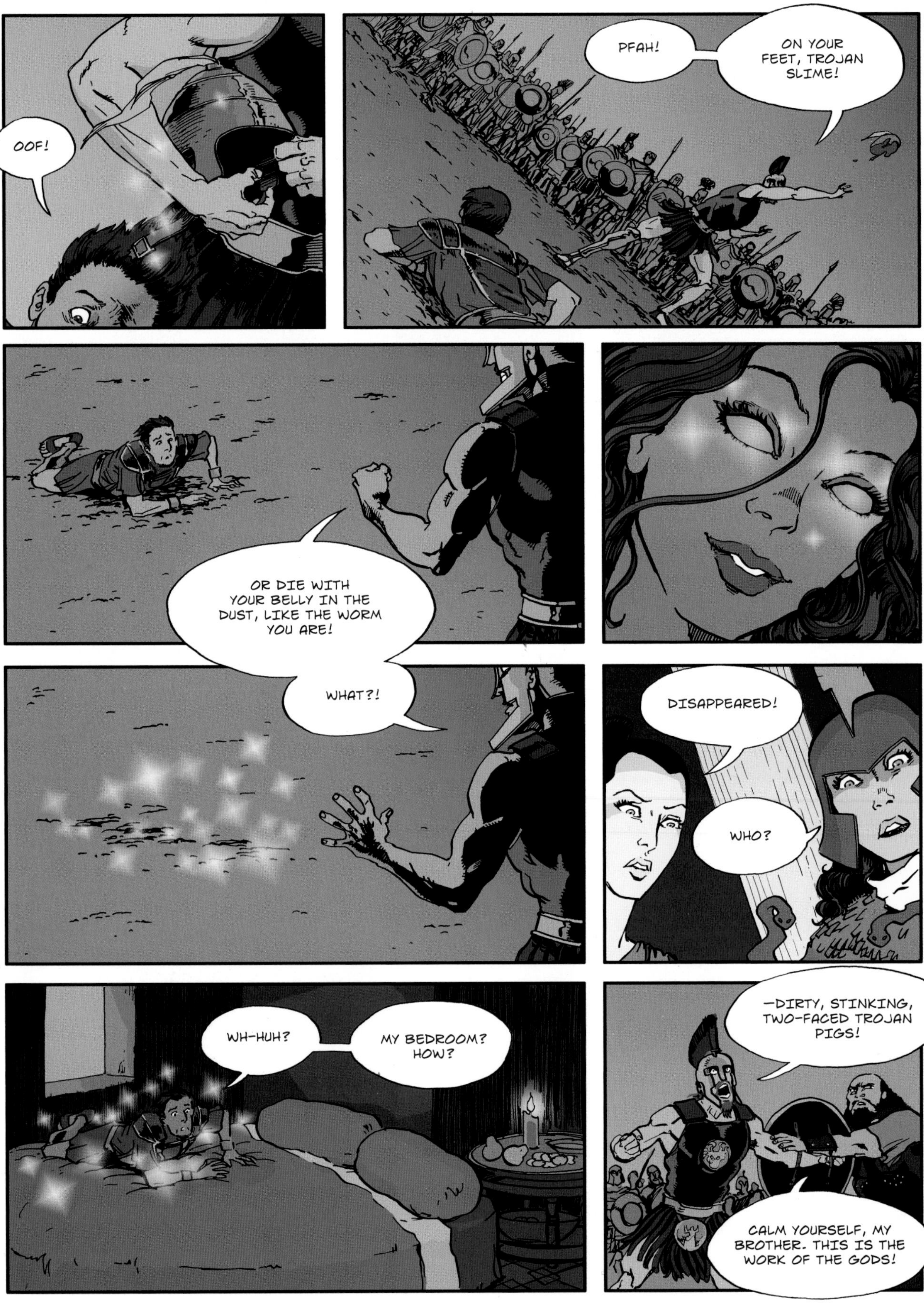
OOF!
PFAH!
ON YOUR FEET, TROJAN SLIME!
OR DIE WITH YOUR BELLY IN THE DUST, LIKE THE WORM YOU ARE!
WHAT?!
DISAPPEARED!
WHO?
WH-HUH?
MY BEDROOM? HOW?
—DIRTY, STINKING, TWO-FACED TROJAN PIGS!
CALM YOURSELF, MY BROTHER. THIS IS THE WORK OF THE GODS!

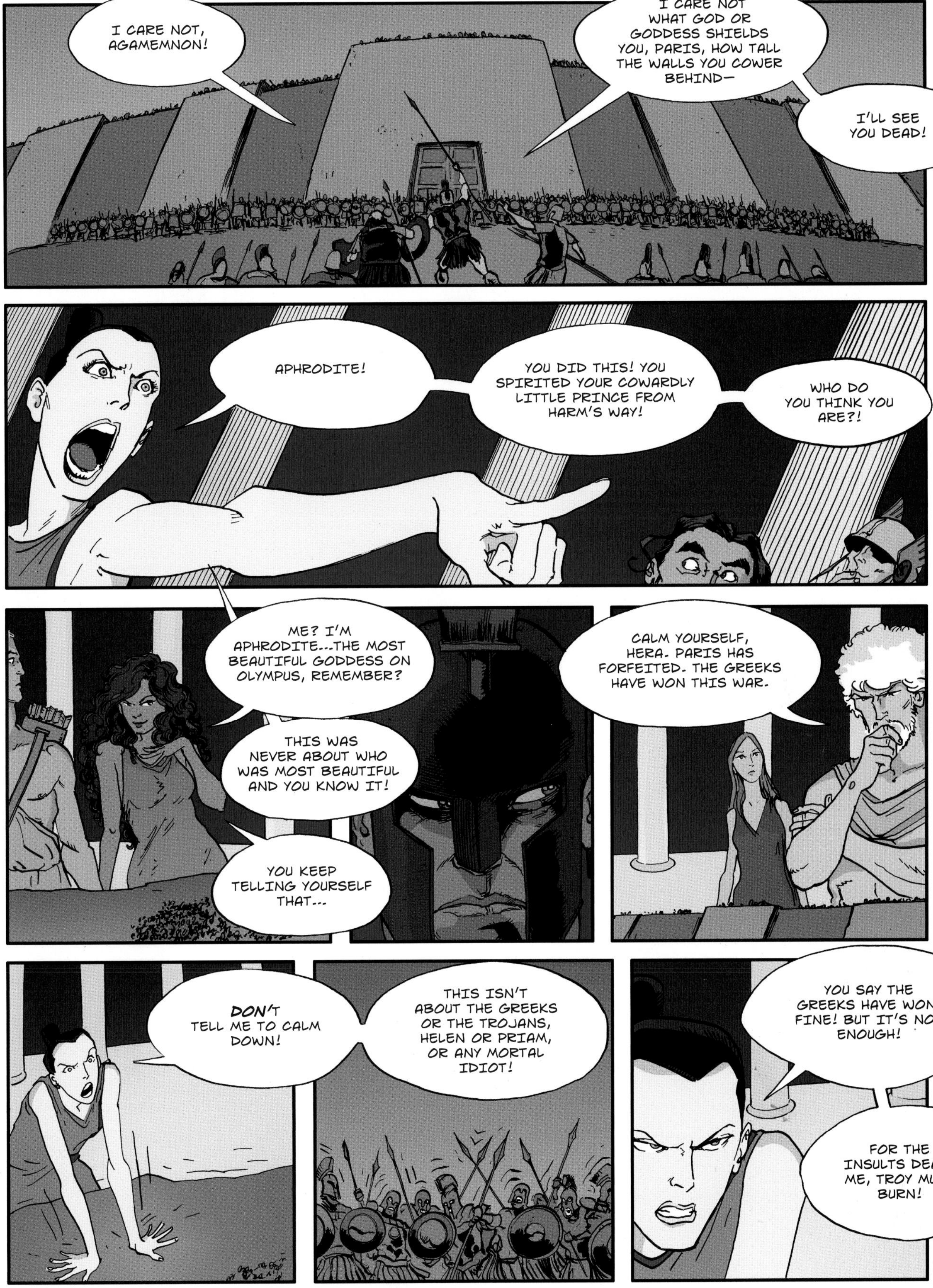
I CARE NOT, AGAMEMNON!
I CARE NOT WHAT GOD OR GODDESS SHIELDS YOU, PARIS, HOW TALL THE WALLS YOU COWER BEHIND—
I'LL SEE YOU DEAD!
APHRODITE!
YOU DID THIS! YOU SPIRITED YOUR COWARDLY LITTLE PRINCE FROM HARM'S WAY!
WHO DO YOU THINK YOU ARE?!
ME? I'M APHRODITE...THE MOST BEAUTIFUL GODDESS ON OLYMPUS, REMEMBER?
THIS WAS NEVER ABOUT WHO WAS MOST BEAUTIFUL AND YOU KNOW IT!
YOU KEEP TELLING YOURSELF THAT...
CALM YOURSELF, HERA. PARIS HAS FORFEITED. THE GREEKS HAVE WON THIS WAR.
DON'T TELL ME TO CALM DOWN!
THIS ISN'T ABOUT THE GREEKS OR THE TROJANS, HELEN OR PRIAM, OR ANY MORTAL IDIOT!
YOU SAY THE GREEKS HAVE WON, FINE! BUT IT'S NOT ENOUGH!
FOR THE INSULTS DEALT ME, TROY MUST BURN!

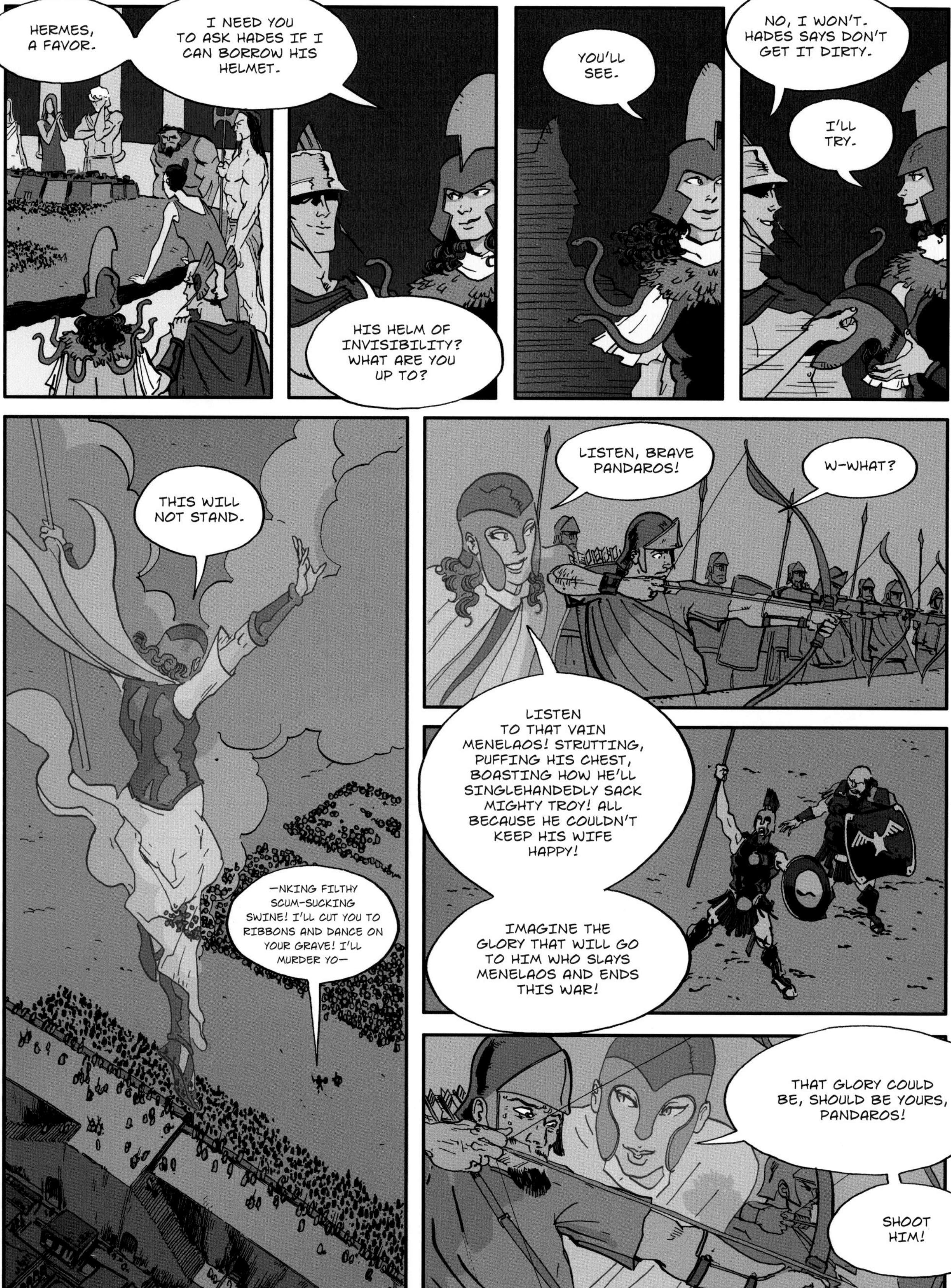
HERMES, A FAVOR.
I NEED YOU TO ASK HADES IF I CAN BORROW HIS HELMET.
HIS HELM OF INVISIBILITY? WHAT ARE YOU UP TO?
YOU'LL SEE.
NO, I WON'T. HADES SAYS DON'T GET IT DIRTY.
I'LL TRY.
THIS WILL NOT STAND.
—NKING FILTHY SCUM-SUCKING SWINE! I'LL CUT YOU TO RIBBONS AND DANCE ON YOUR GRAVE! I'LL MURDER YO—
LISTEN, BRAVE PANDAROS!
W-WHAT?
LISTEN TO THAT VAIN MENELAOS! STRUTTING, PUFFING HIS CHEST, BOASTING HOW HE'LL SINGLEHANDEDLY SACK MIGHTY TROY! ALL BECAUSE HE COULDN'T KEEP HIS WIFE HAPPY!
IMAGINE THE GLORY THAT WILL GO TO HIM WHO SLAYS MENELAOS AND ENDS THIS WAR!
THAT GLORY COULD BE, SHOULD BE YOURS, PANDAROS!
SHOOT HIM!

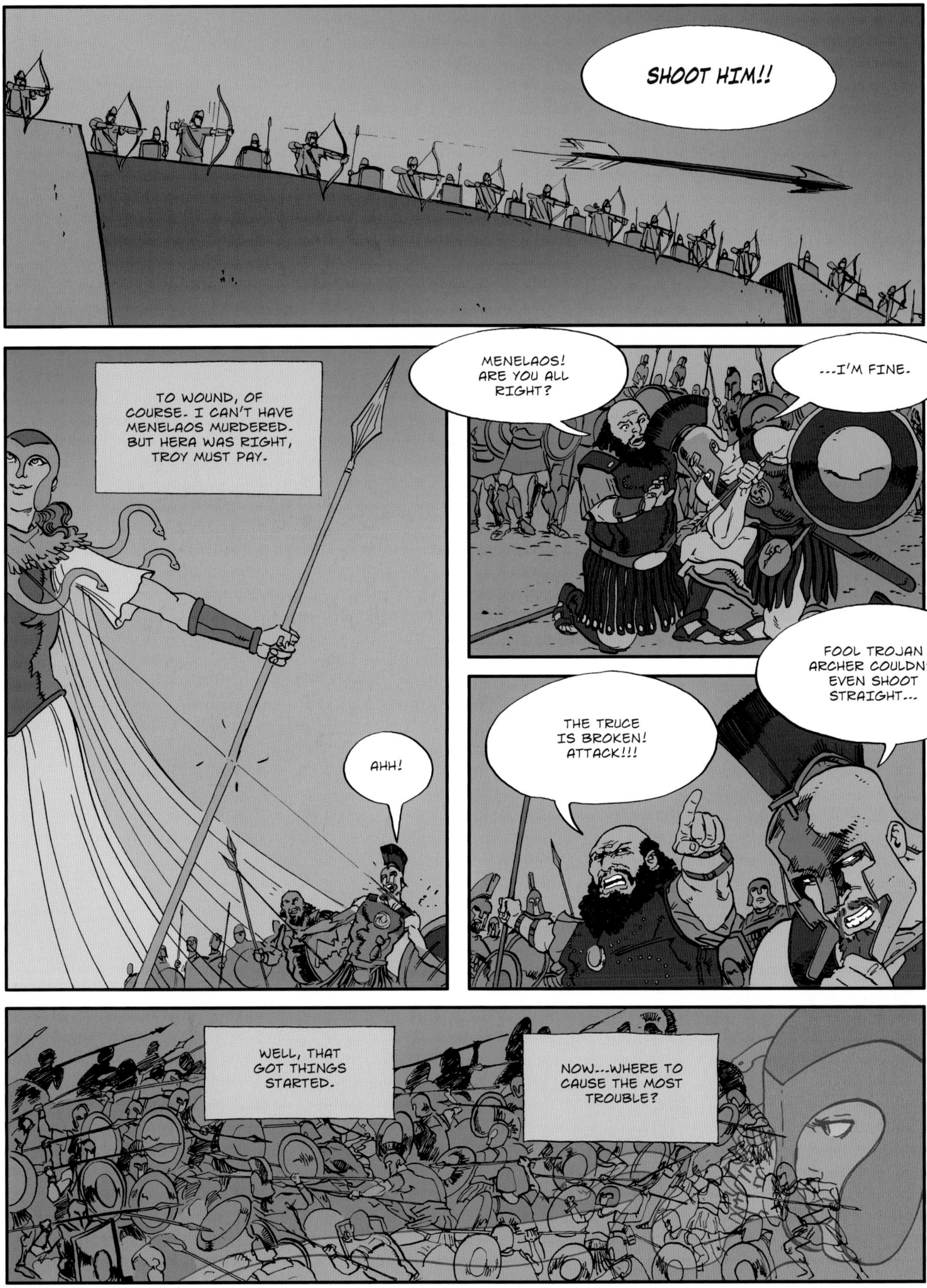

SHOOT HIM!!
TO WOUND, OF COURSE. I CAN'T HAVE MENELAOS MURDERED. BUT HERA WAS RIGHT, TROY MUST PAY.
AHH!
MENELAOS! ARE YOU ALL RIGHT?
---I'M FINE.
FOOL TROJAN ARCHER COULDN'T EVEN SHOOT STRAIGHT---
THE TRUCE IS BROKEN! ATTACK!!!
WELL, THAT GOT THINGS STARTED.
NOW---WHERE TO CAUSE THE MOST TROUBLE?

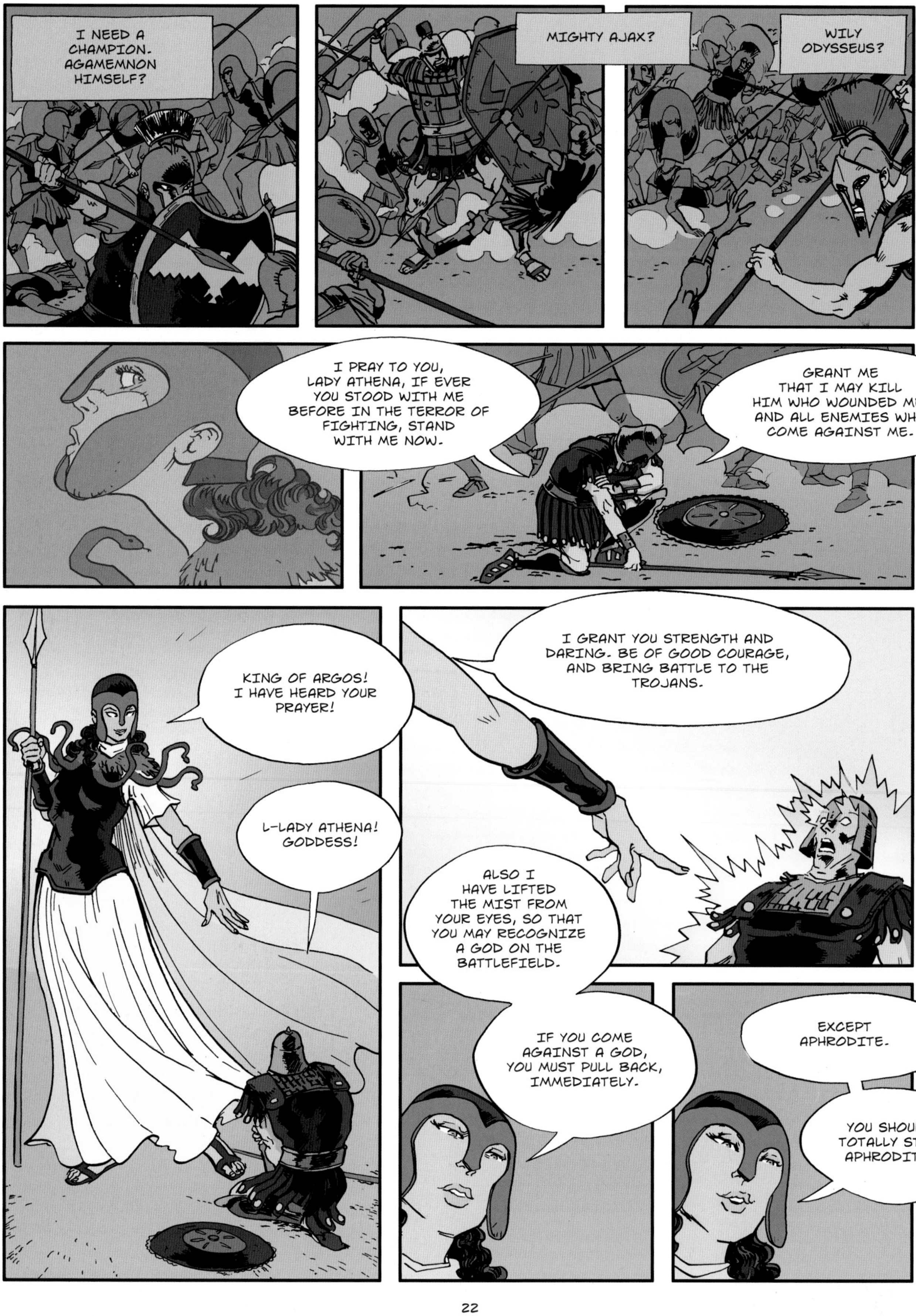
I NEED A CHAMPION. AGAMEMNON HIMSELF?
MIGHTY AJAX?
WILY ODYSSEUS?
I PRAY TO YOU, LADY ATHENA, IF EVER YOU STOOD WITH ME BEFORE IN THE TERROR OF FIGHTING, STAND WITH ME NOW.
GRANT ME THAT I MAY KILL HIM WHO WOUNDED ME, AND ALL ENEMIES WHO COME AGAINST ME.
KING OF ARGOS! I HAVE HEARD YOUR PRAYER!
L-LADY ATHENA! GODDESS!
I GRANT YOU STRENGTH AND DARING. BE OF GOOD COURAGE, AND BRING BATTLE TO THE TROJANS.
ALSO I HAVE LIFTED THE MIST FROM YOUR EYES, SO THAT YOU MAY RECOGNIZE A GOD ON THE BATTLEFIELD.
IF YOU COME AGAINST A GOD, YOU MUST PULL BACK, IMMEDIATELY.
EXCEPT APHRODITE.
YOU SHOULD TOTALLY STAB APHRODITE.

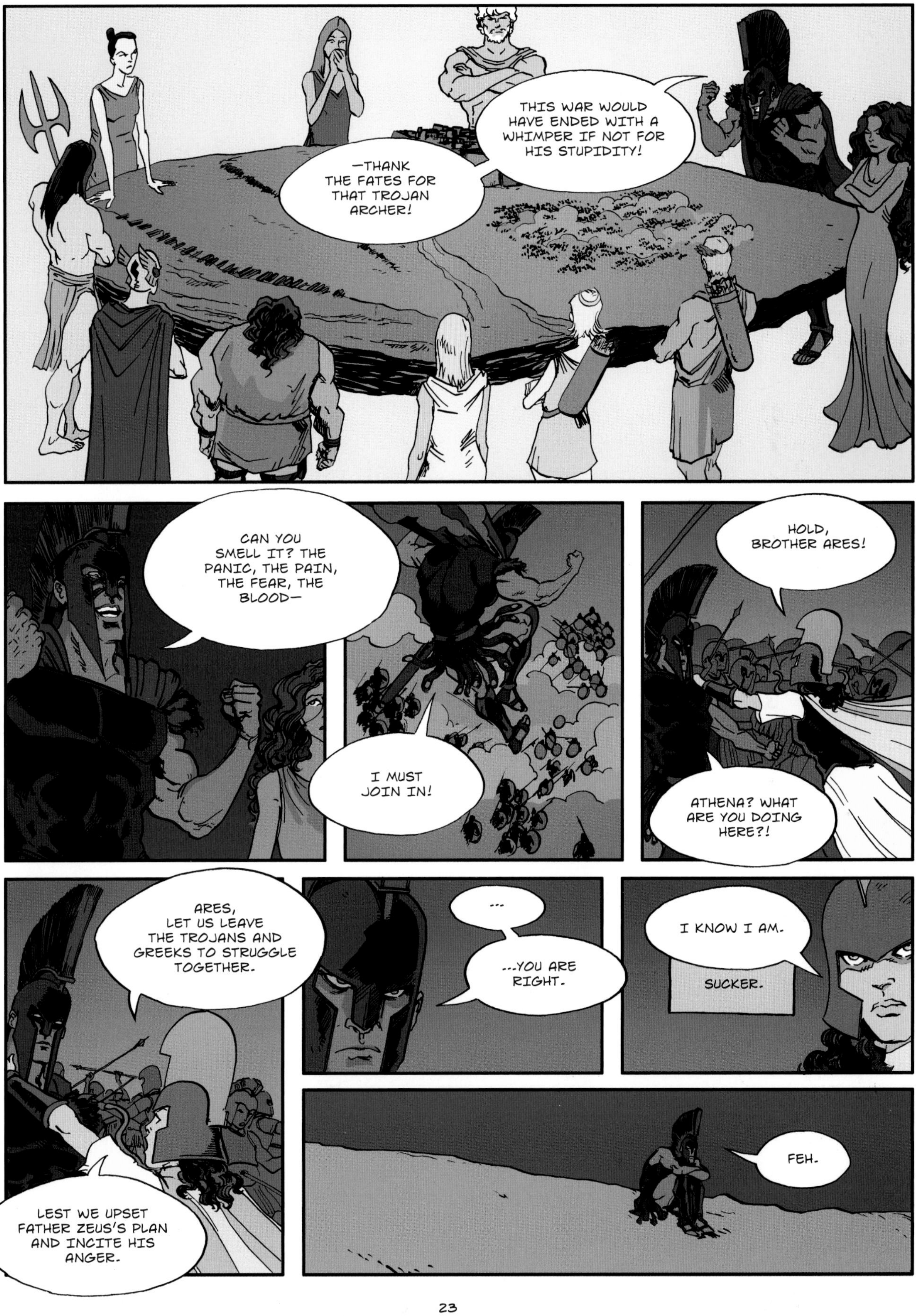
—THANK THE FATES FOR THAT TROJAN ARCHER!
THIS WAR WOULD HAVE ENDED WITH A WHIMPER IF NOT FOR HIS STUPIDITY!
CAN YOU SMELL IT? THE PANIC, THE PAIN, THE FEAR, THE BLOOD—
I MUST JOIN IN!
HOLD, BROTHER ARES!
ATHENA? WHAT ARE YOU DOING HERE?!
ARES, LET US LEAVE THE TROJANS AND GREEKS TO STRUGGLE TOGETHER.
LEST WE UPSET FATHER ZEUS'S PLAN AND INCITE HIS ANGER.
...
...YOU ARE RIGHT.
I KNOW I AM.
SUCKER.
FEH.

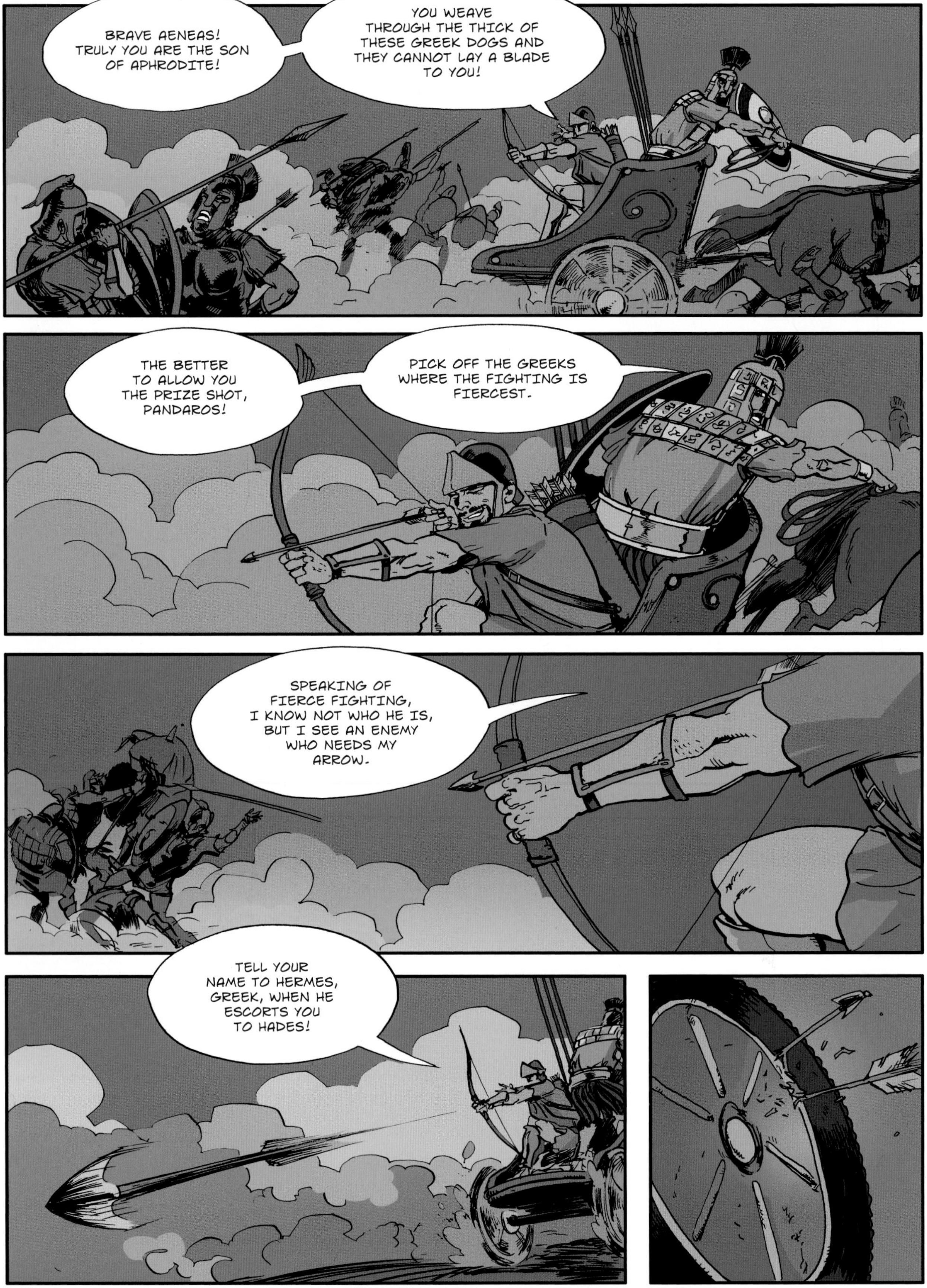
BRAVE AENEAS! TRULY YOU ARE THE SON OF APHRODITE!
YOU WEAVE THROUGH THE THICK OF THESE GREEK DOGS AND THEY CANNOT LAY A BLADE TO YOU!
THE BETTER TO ALLOW YOU THE PRIZE SHOT, PANDAROS!
PICK OFF THE GREEKS WHERE THE FIGHTING IS FIERCEST.
SPEAKING OF FIERCE FIGHTING, I KNOW NOT WHO HE IS, BUT I SEE AN ENEMY WHO NEEDS MY ARROW.
TELL YOUR NAME TO HERMES, GREEK, WHEN HE ESCORTS YOU TO HADES!

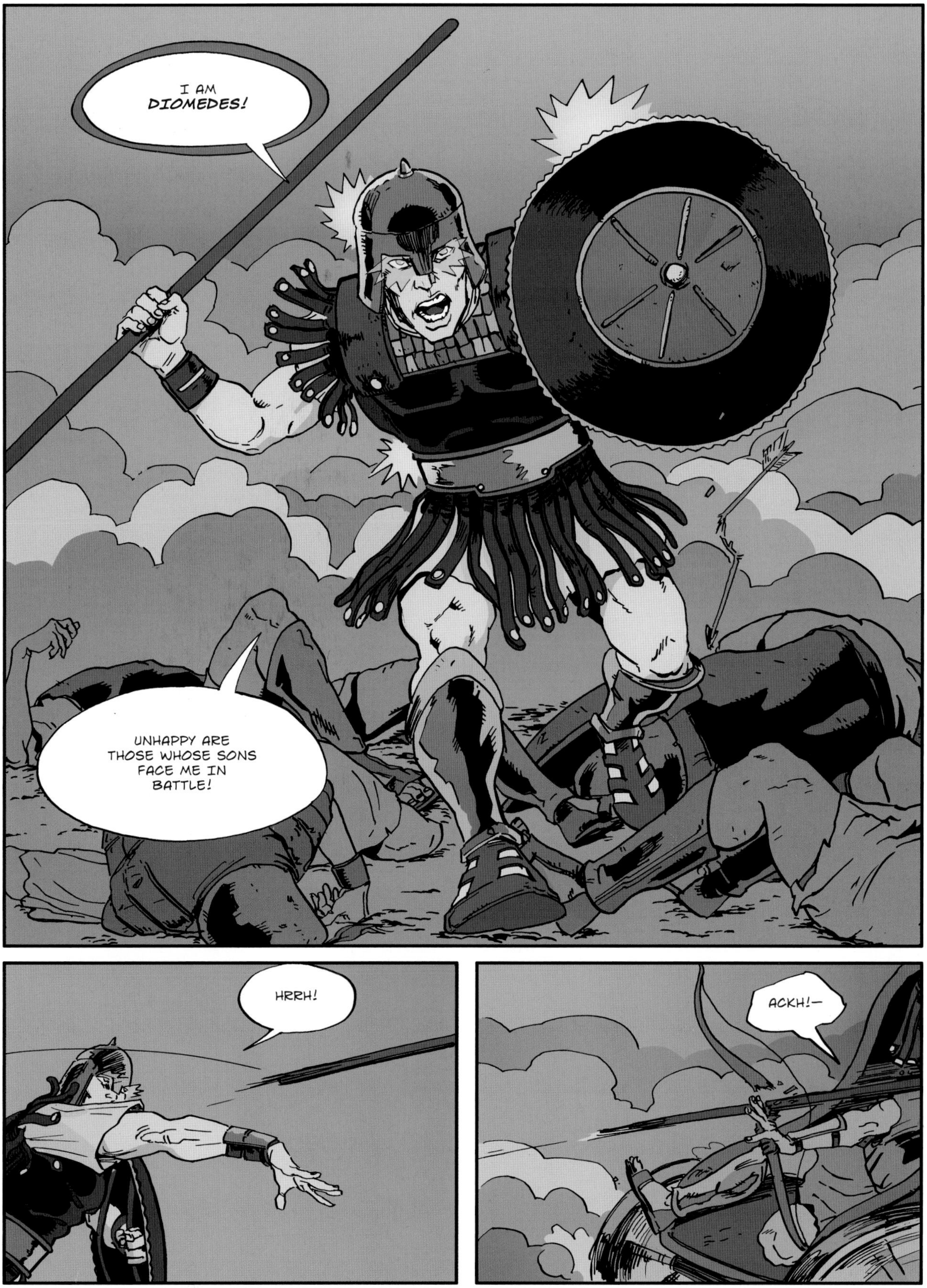
I AM DIOMEDES!
UNHAPPY ARE THOSE WHOSE SONS FACE ME IN BATTLE!
HRRH!
ACKH!—

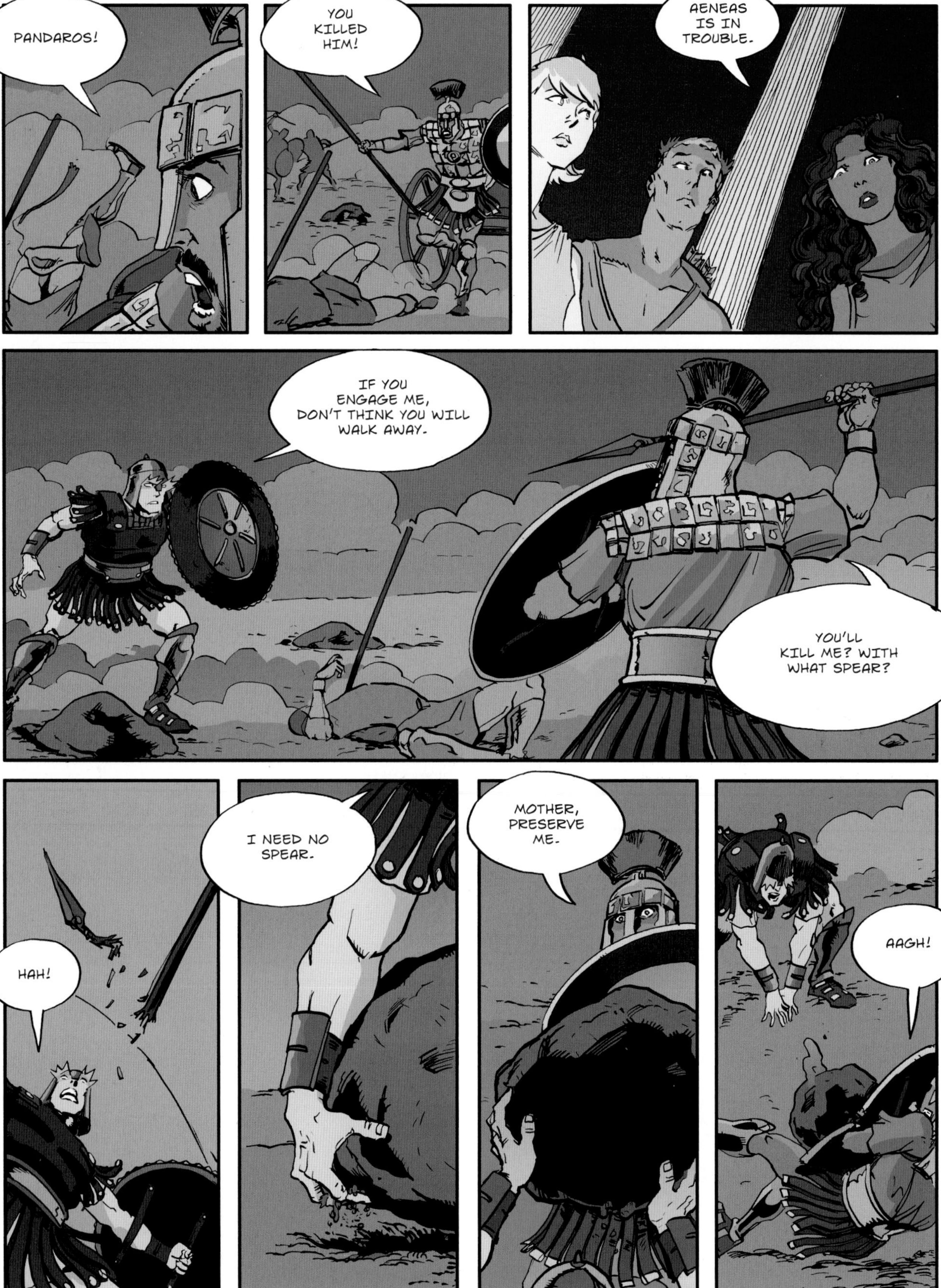
PANDAROS!
YOU KILLED HIM!
AENEAS IS IN TROUBLE.
IF YOU ENGAGE ME, DON'T THINK YOU WILL WALK AWAY.
YOU'LL KILL ME? WITH WHAT SPEAR?
HAH!
I NEED NO SPEAR.
MOTHER, PRESERVE ME.
AAGH!

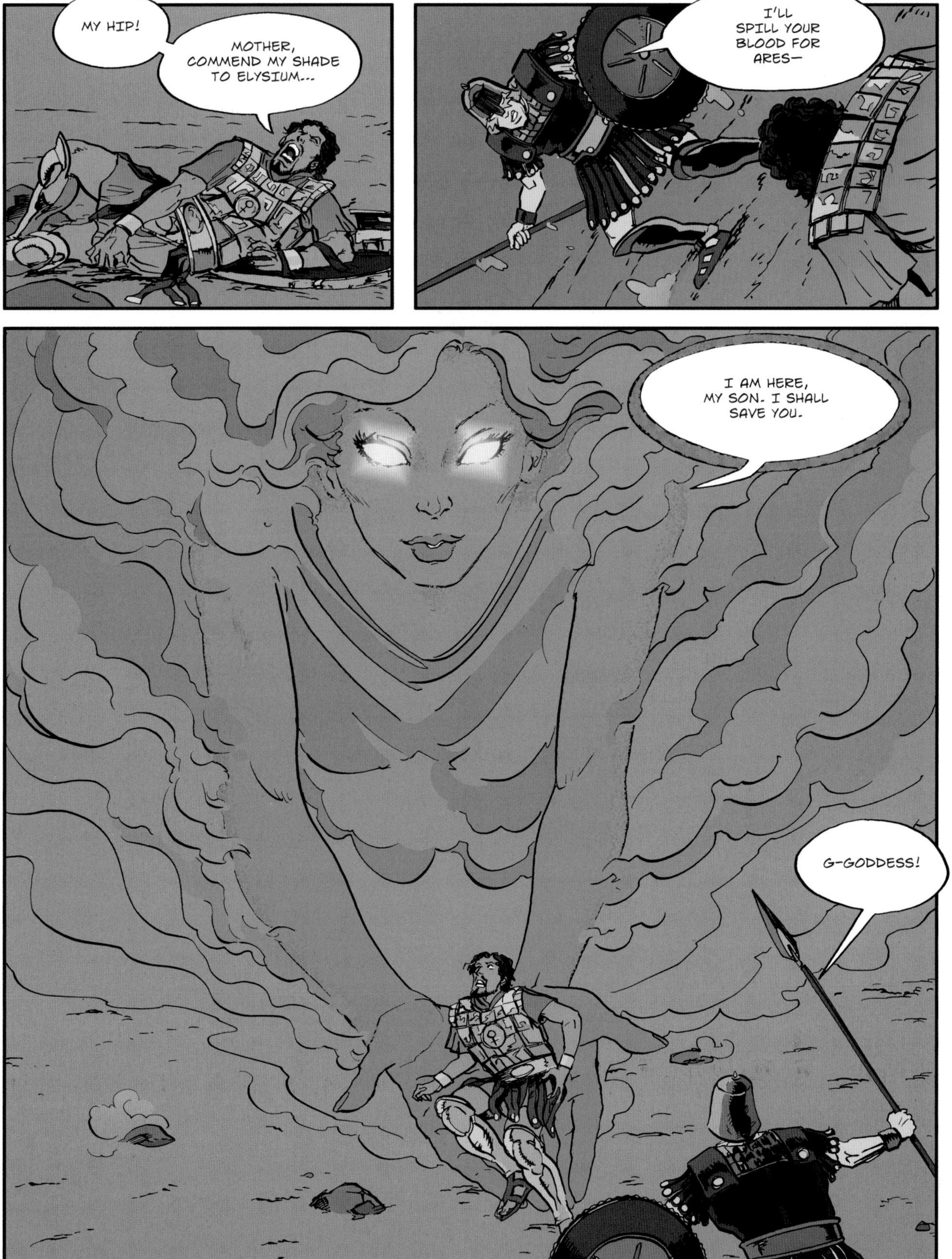
MY HIP!
MOTHER, COMMEND MY SHADE TO ELYSIUM...
I'LL SPILL YOUR BLOOD FOR ARES—
I AM HERE, MY SON. I SHALL SAVE YOU.
G-GODDESS!

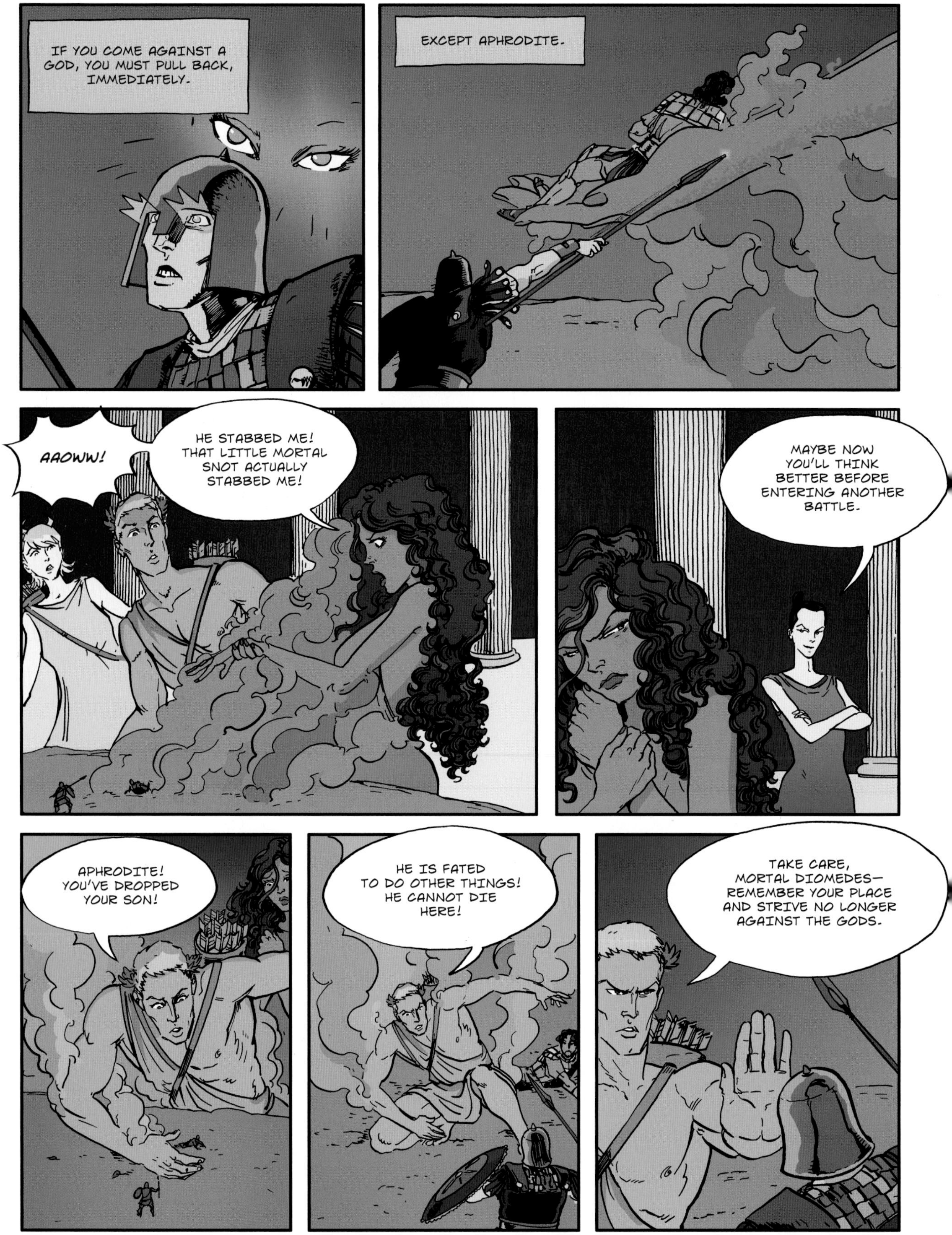

IF YOU COME AGAINST A GOD, YOU MUST PULL BACK, IMMEDIATELY.
EXCEPT APHRODITE.
AAOWW!
HE STABBED ME! THAT LITTLE MORTAL SNOT ACTUALLY STABBED ME!
MAYBE NOW YOU'LL THINK BETTER BEFORE ENTERING ANOTHER BATTLE.
APHRODITE! YOU'VE DROPPED YOUR SON!
HE IS FATED TO DO OTHER THINGS! HE CANNOT DIE HERE!
TAKE CARE, MORTAL DIOMEDES— REMEMBER YOUR PLACE AND STRIVE NO LONGER AGAINST THE GODS.

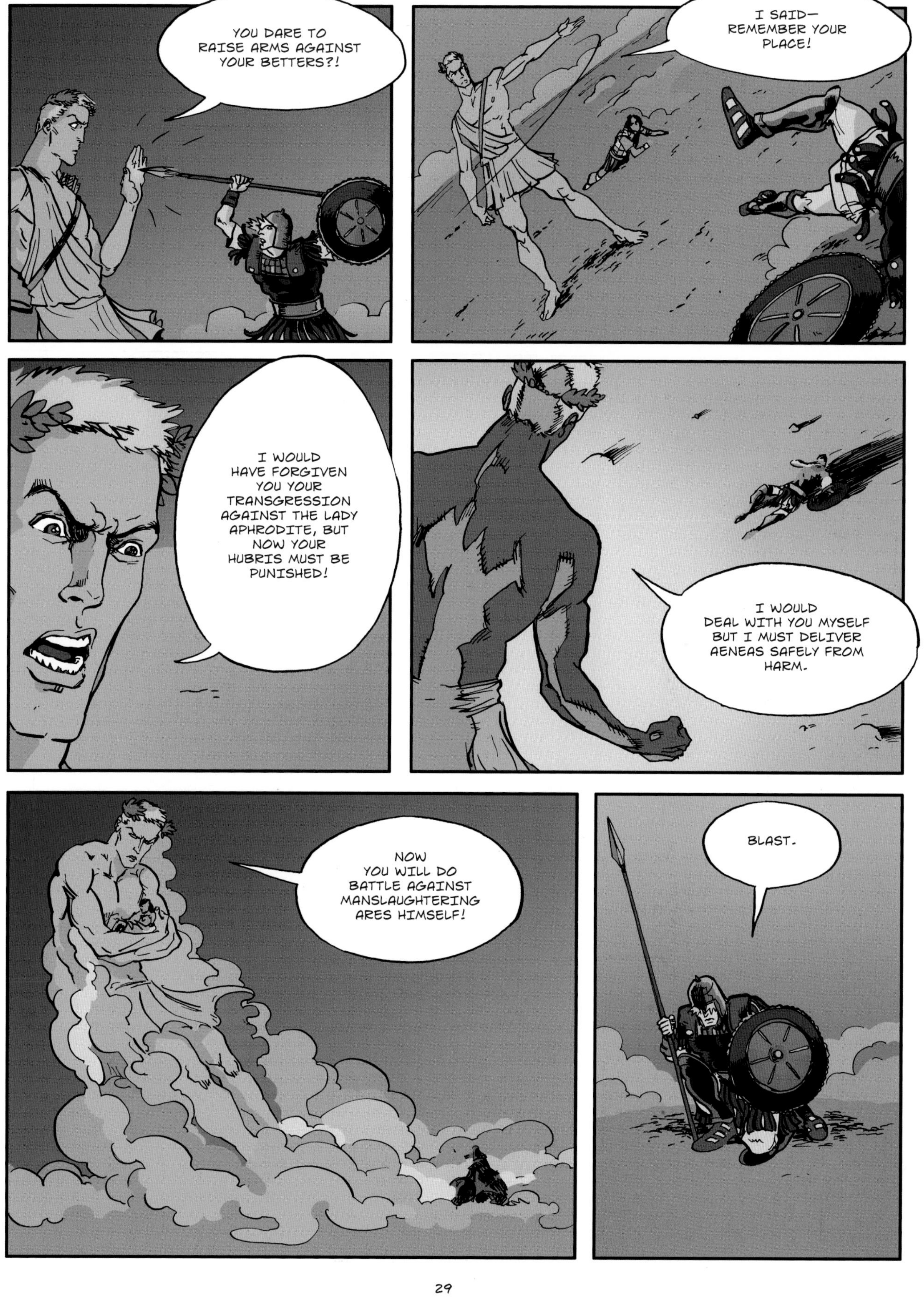
YOU DARE TO RAISE ARMS AGAINST YOUR BETTERS?!
I SAID— REMEMBER YOUR PLACE!
I WOULD HAVE FORGIVEN YOU YOUR TRANSGRESSION AGAINST THE LADY APHRODITE, BUT NOW YOUR HUBRIS MUST BE PUNISHED!
I WOULD DEAL WITH YOU MYSELF BUT I MUST DELIVER AENEAS SAFELY FROM HARM.
NOW YOU WILL DO BATTLE AGAINST MANSLAUGHTERING ARES HIMSELF!
BLAST.

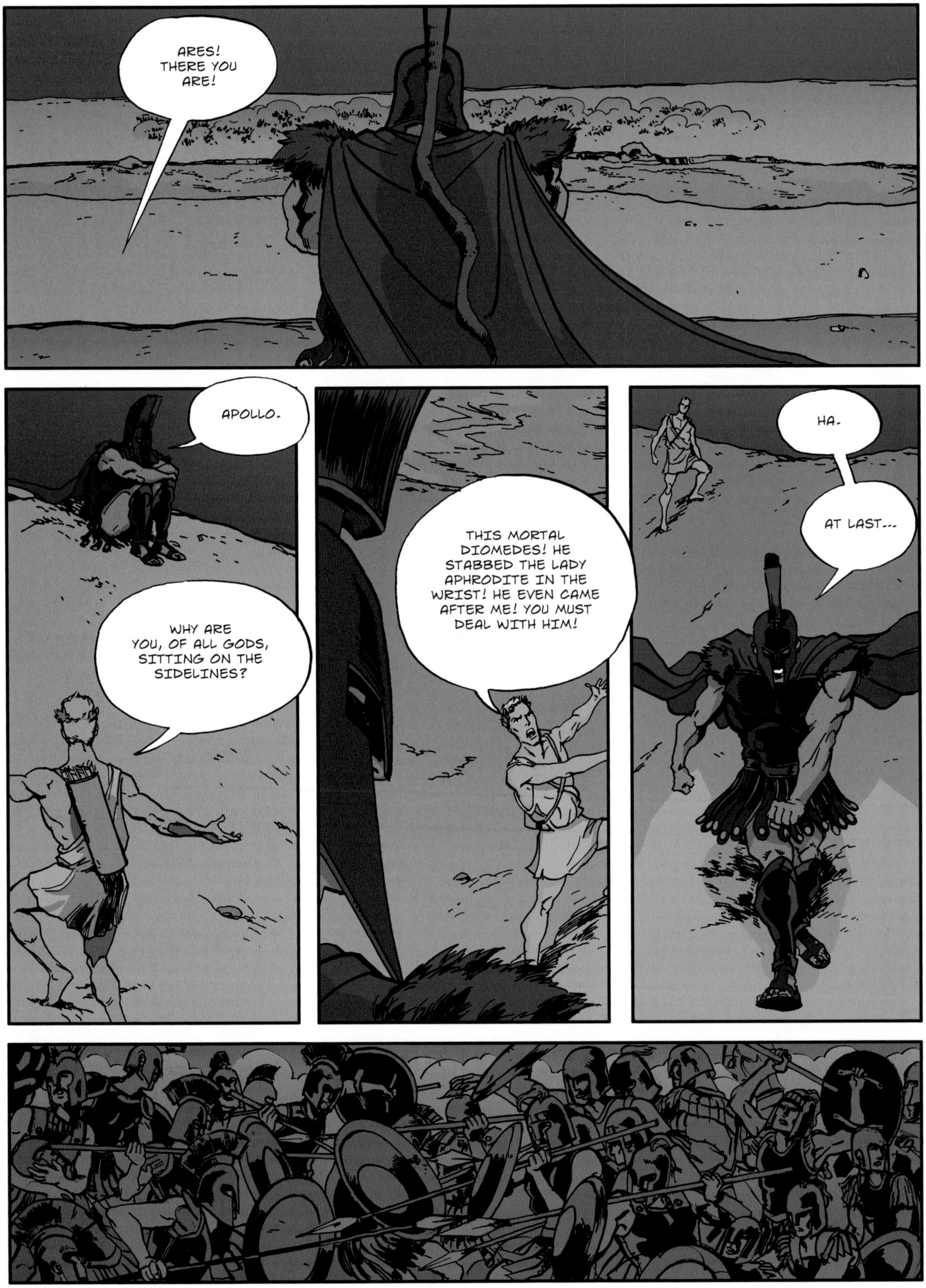
ARES! THERE YOU ARE!
APOLLO.
WHY ARE YOU, OF ALL GODS, SITTING ON THE SIDELINES?
THIS MORTAL DIOMEDES! HE STABBED THE LADY APHRODITE IN THE WRIST! HE EVEN CAME AFTER ME! YOU MUST DEAL WITH HIM!
HA.
AT LAST...

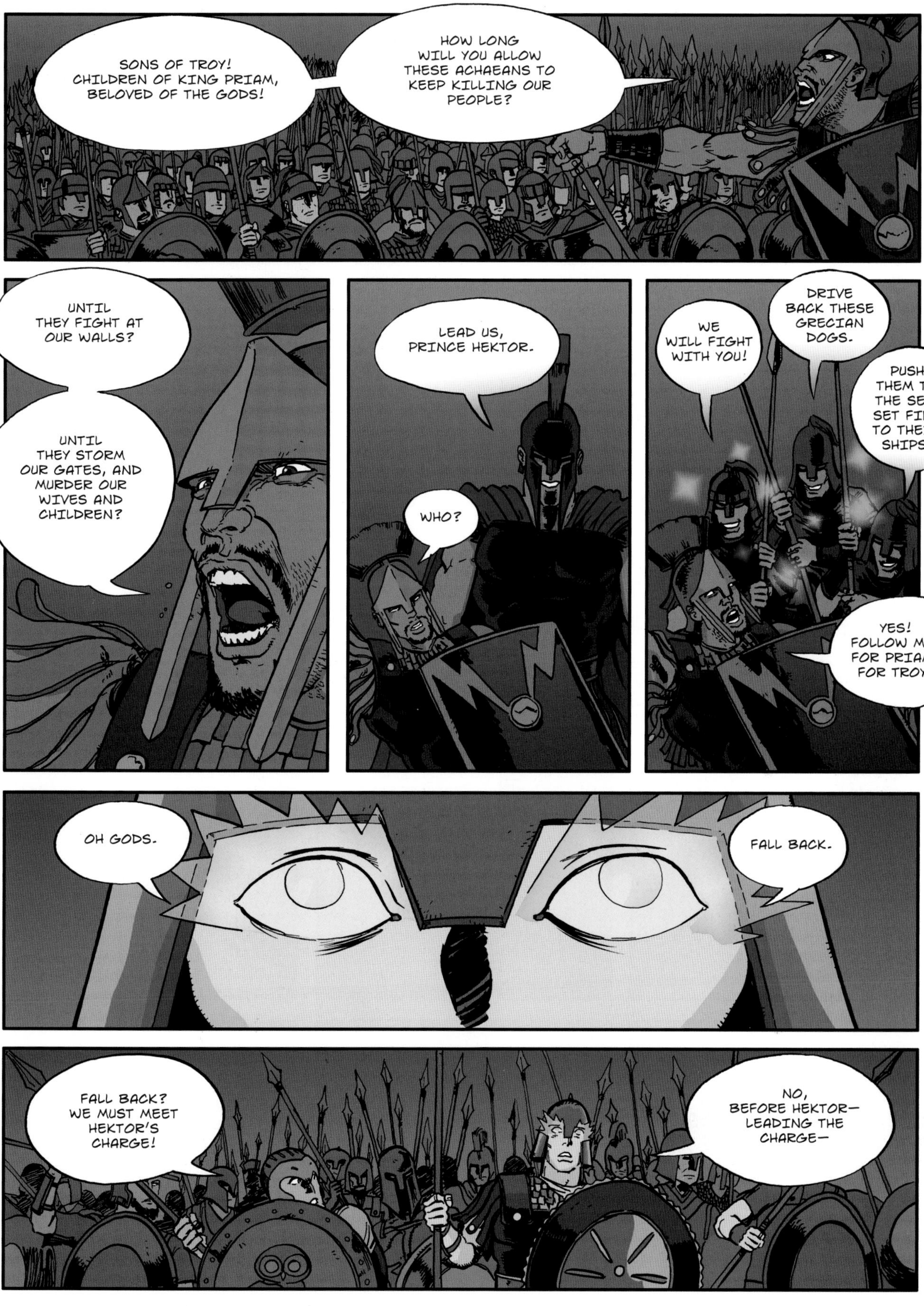
SONS OF TROY! CHILDREN OF KING PRIAM, BELOVED OF THE GODS!
HOW LONG WILL YOU ALLOW THESE ACHAEANS TO KEEP KILLING OUR PEOPLE?
UNTIL THEY FIGHT AT OUR WALLS?
UNTIL THEY STORM OUR GATES, AND MURDER OUR WIVES AND CHILDREN?
LEAD US, PRINCE HEKTOR.
WHO?
WE WILL FIGHT WITH YOU!
DRIVE BACK THESE GRECIAN DOGS.
PUSH THEM TO THE SEA, SET FIRE TO THEIR SHIPS.
YES! FOLLOW ME! FOR PRIAM! FOR TROY!
OH GODS.
FALL BACK.
FALL BACK? WE MUST MEET HEKTOR'S CHARGE!
NO, BEFORE HEKTOR— LEADING THE CHARGE—

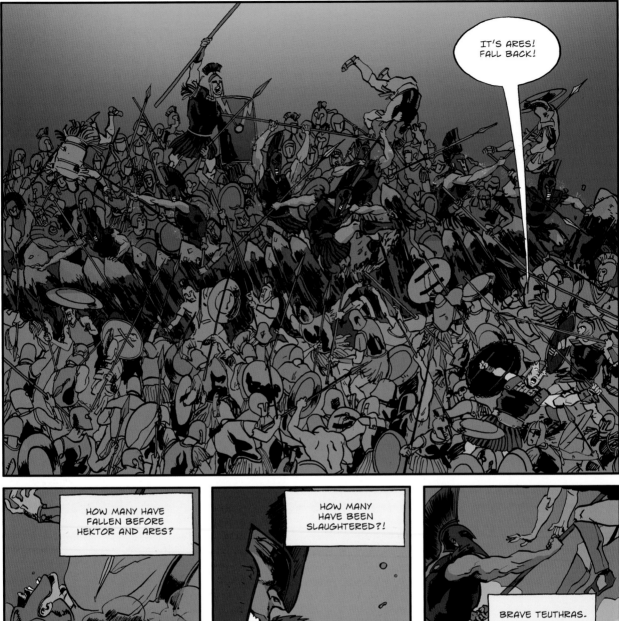

IT'S ARES! FALL BACK!

HOW MANY HAVE FALLEN BEFORE HEKTOR AND ARES?

HOW MANY HAVE BEEN SLAUGHTERED?!

BRAVE TEUTHRAS.

MIGHTY ORESTES.

NOBLE TRECHOS.

SHINING HELENOS.

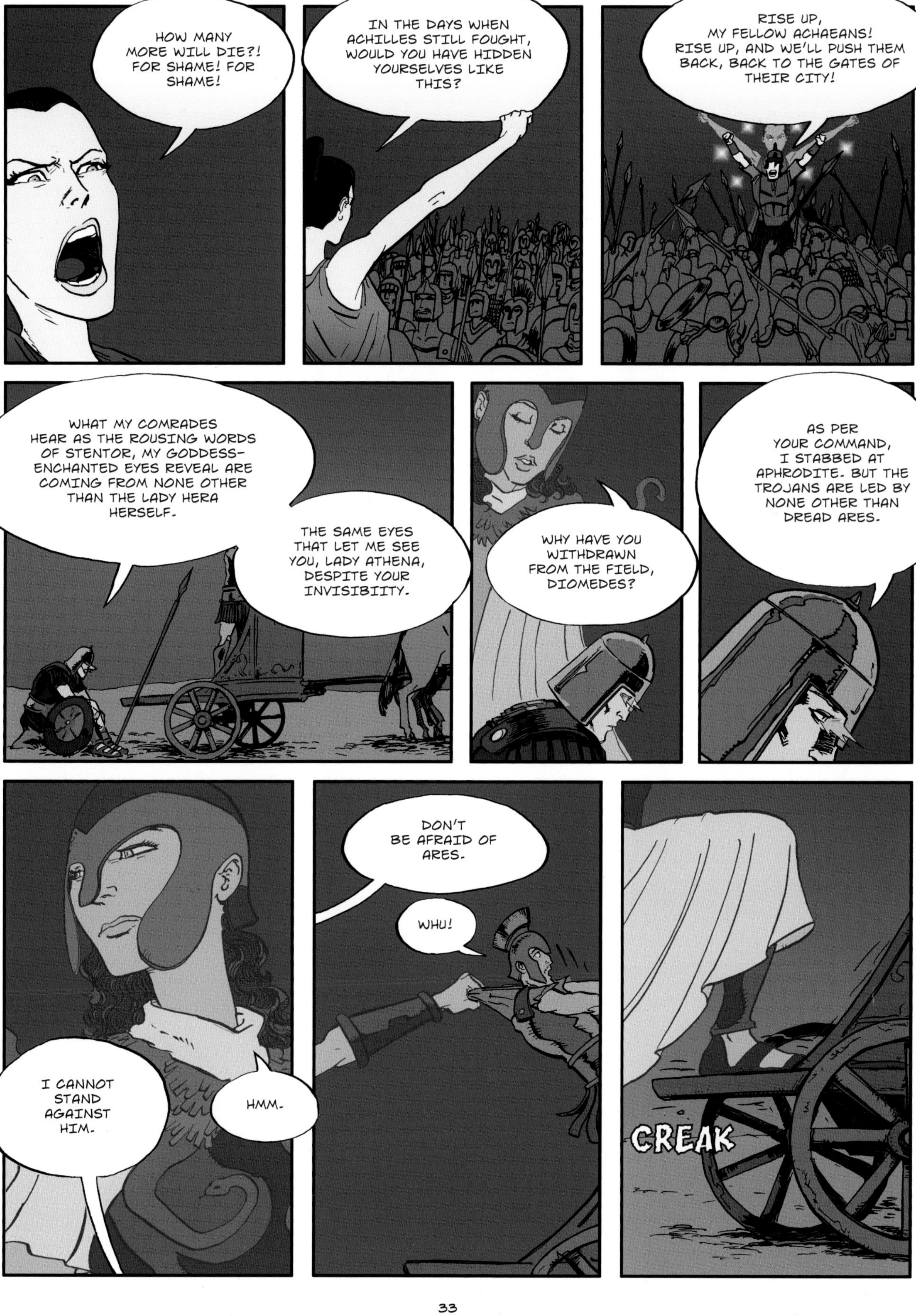
HOW MANY MORE WILL DIE?! FOR SHAME! FOR SHAME!
IN THE DAYS WHEN ACHILLES STILL FOUGHT, WOULD YOU HAVE HIDDEN YOURSELVES LIKE THIS?
RISE UP, MY FELLOW ACHAEANS! RISE UP, AND WE'LL PUSH THEM BACK, BACK TO THE GATES OF THEIR CITY!
WHAT MY COMRADES HEAR AS THE ROUSING WORDS OF STENTOR, MY GODDESS-ENCHANTED EYES REVEAL ARE COMING FROM NONE OTHER THAN THE LADY HERA HERSELF.
THE SAME EYES THAT LET ME SEE YOU, LADY ATHENA, DESPITE YOUR INVISIBIITY.
WHY HAVE YOU WITHDRAWN FROM THE FIELD, DIOMEDES?
AS PER YOUR COMMAND, I STABBED AT APHRODITE. BUT THE TROJANS ARE LED BY NONE OTHER THAN DREAD ARES.
I CANNOT STAND AGAINST HIM.
HMM.
DON'T BE AFRAID OF ARES.
WHU!
CREAK

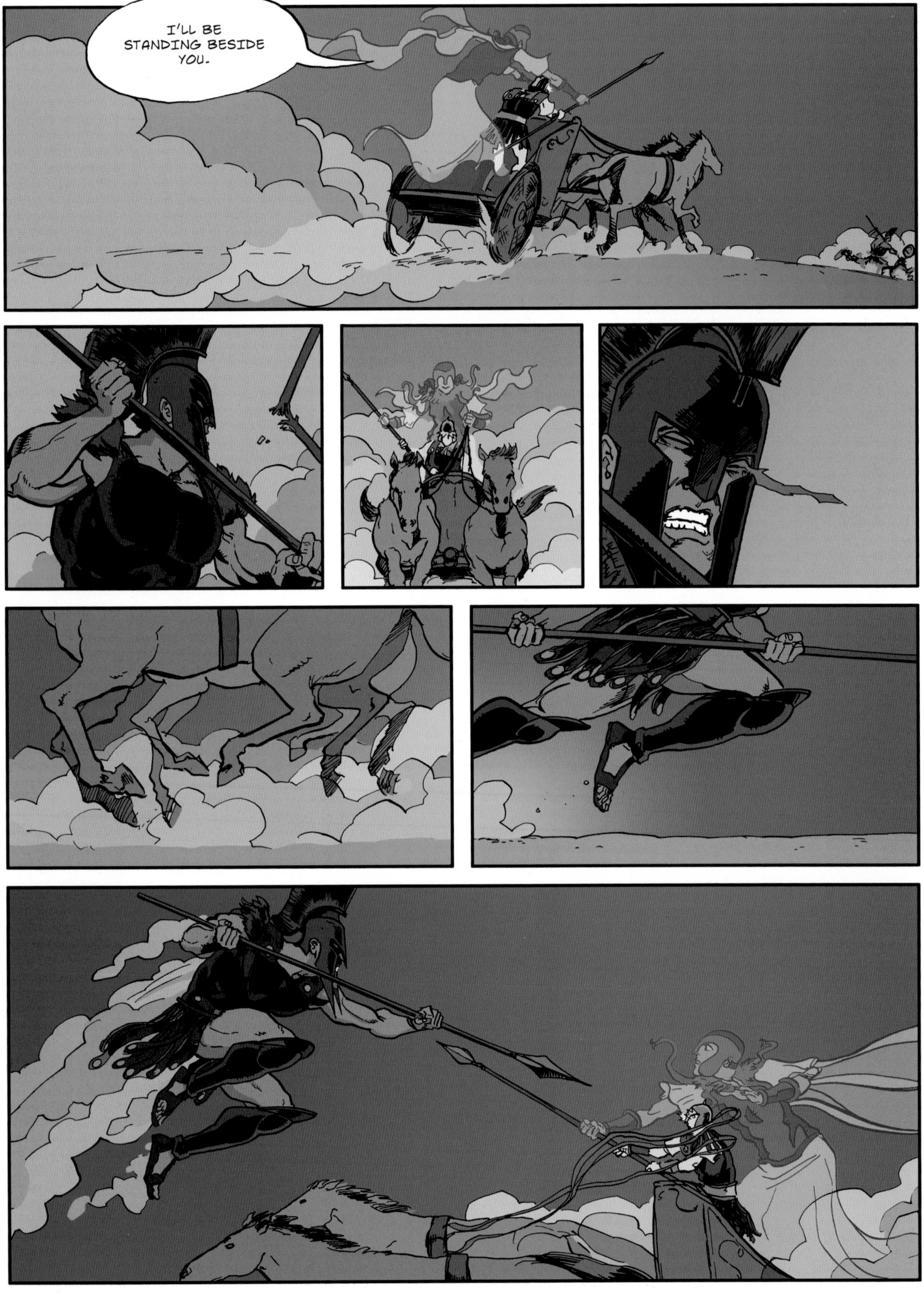
I'LL BE STANDING BESIDE YOU.

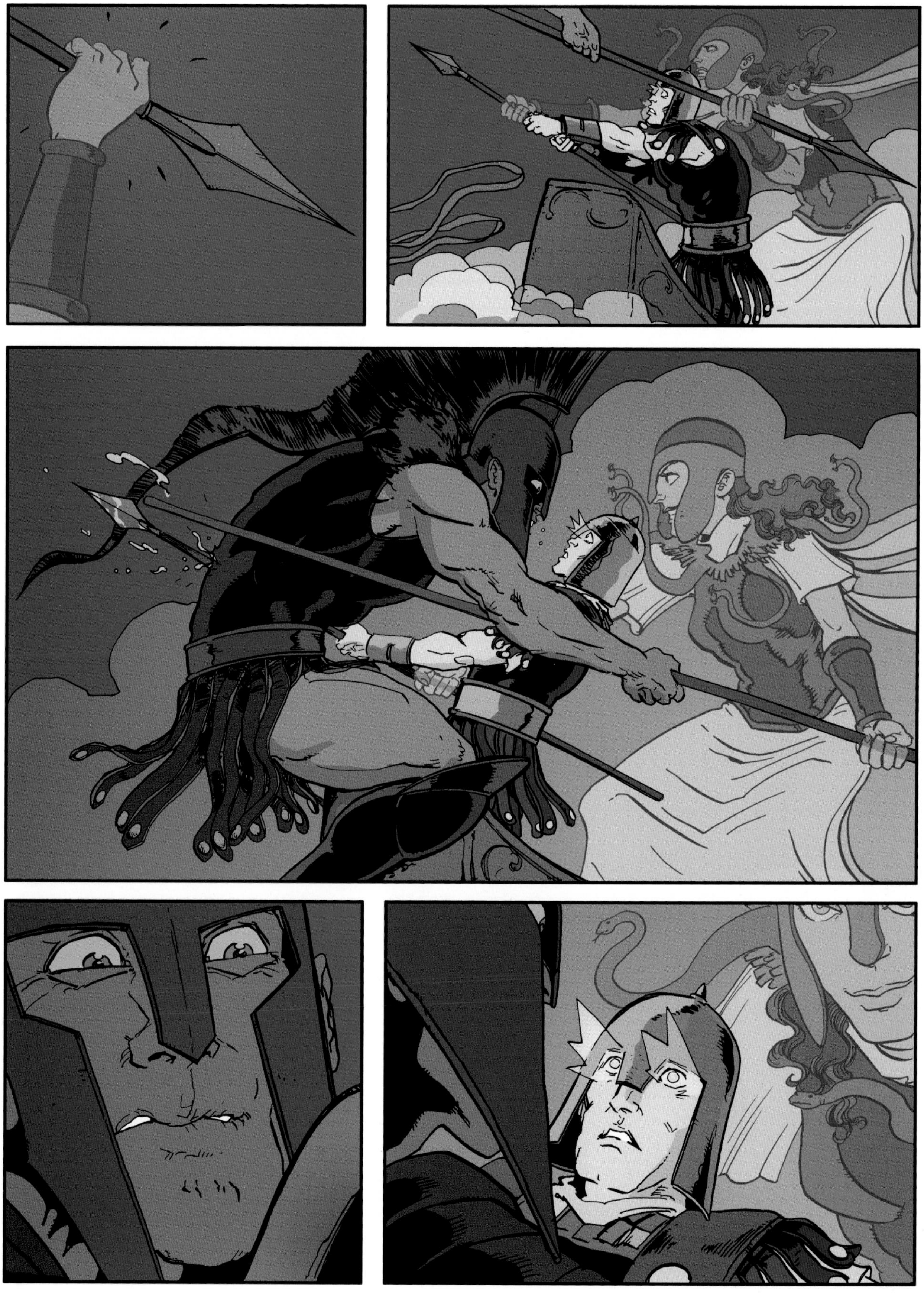

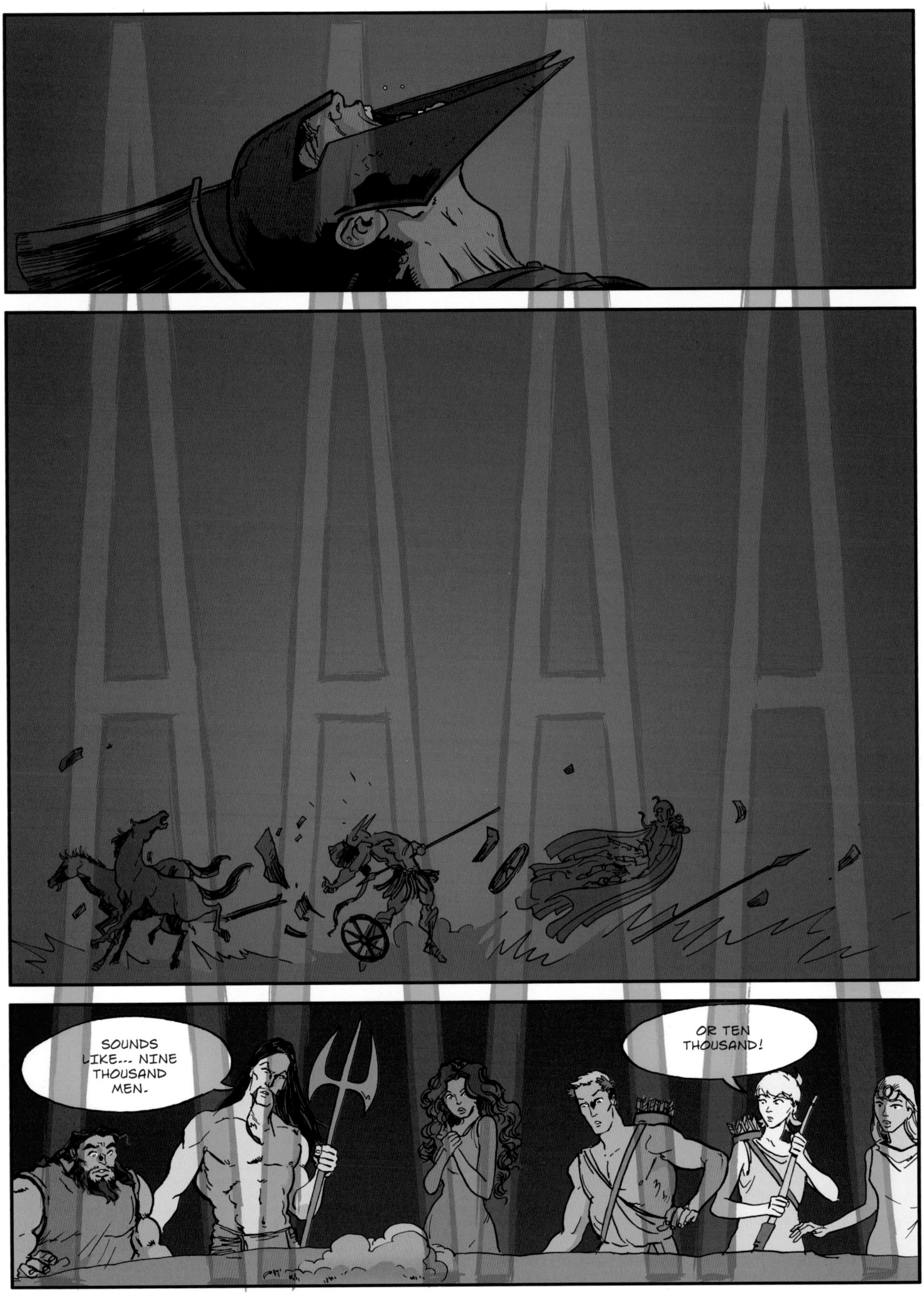
SOUNDS LIKE... NINE THOUSAND MEN.
OR TEN THOUSAND!

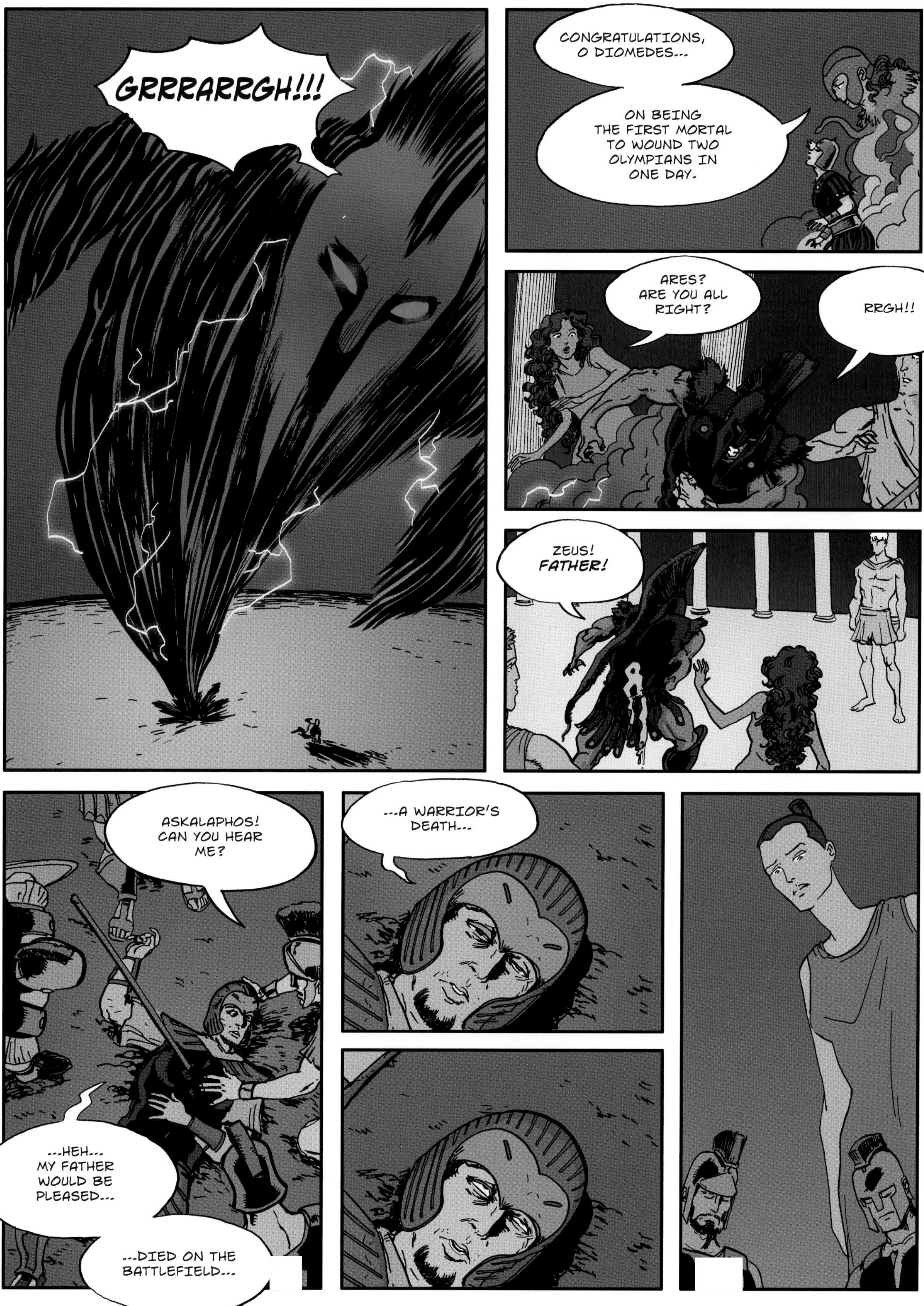
GRRRARRGH!!!
CONGRATULATIONS, O DIOMEDES...
ON BEING THE FIRST MORTAL TO WOUND TWO OLYMPIANS IN ONE DAY.
ARES? ARE YOU ALL RIGHT?
RRGH!!
ZEUS! FATHER!
ASKALAPHOS! CAN YOU HEAR ME?
...HEH... MY FATHER WOULD BE PLEASED...
...DIED ON THE BATTLEFIELD...
...A WARRIOR'S DEATH...

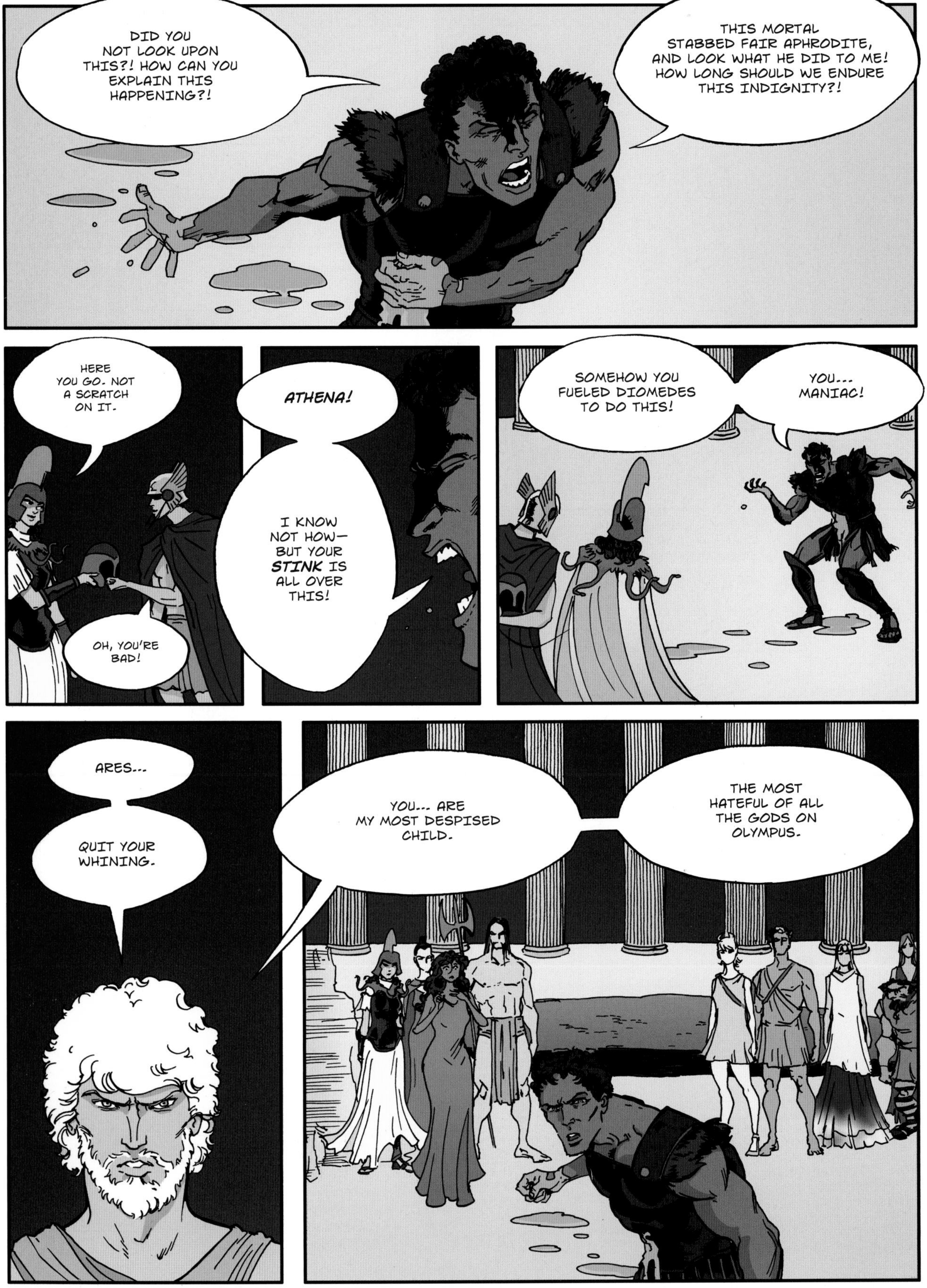
DID YOU NOT LOOK UPON THIS?! HOW CAN YOU EXPLAIN THIS HAPPENING?!
THIS MORTAL STABBED FAIR APHRODITE, AND LOOK WHAT HE DID TO ME! HOW LONG SHOULD WE ENDURE THIS INDIGNITY?!
HERE YOU GO. NOT A SCRATCH ON IT.
OH, YOU'RE BAD!
ATHENA!
I KNOW NOT HOW— BUT YOUR STINK IS ALL OVER THIS!
SOMEHOW YOU FUELED DIOMEDES TO DO THIS!
YOU... MANIAC!
ARES...
QUIT YOUR WHINING.
YOU... ARE MY MOST DESPISED CHILD.
THE MOST HATEFUL OF ALL THE GODS ON OLYMPUS.

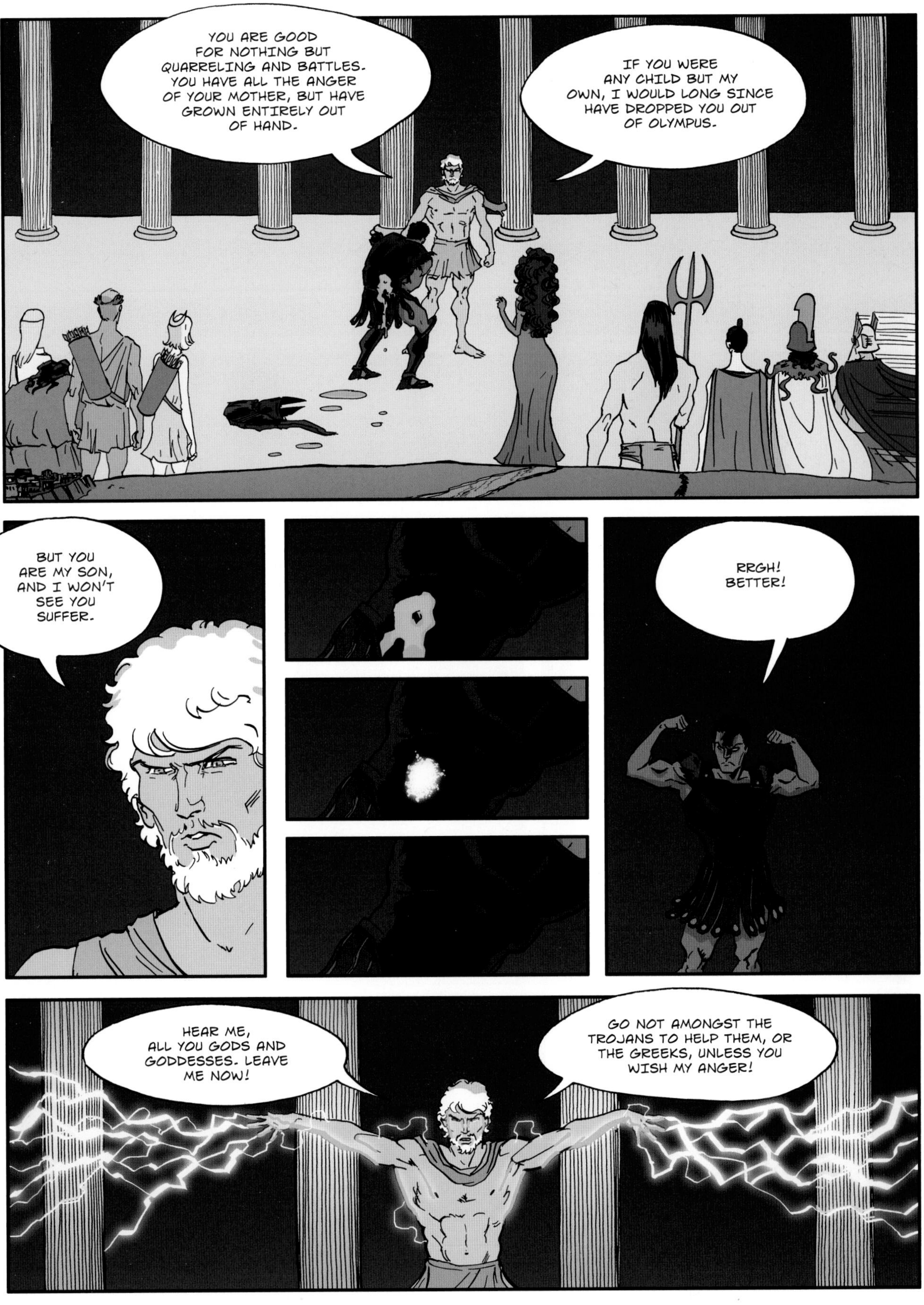
YOU ARE GOOD FOR NOTHING BUT QUARRELING AND BATTLES. YOU HAVE ALL THE ANGER OF YOUR MOTHER, BUT HAVE GROWN ENTIRELY OUT OF HAND.
IF YOU WERE ANY CHILD BUT MY OWN, I WOULD LONG SINCE HAVE DROPPED YOU OUT OF OLYMPUS.
BUT YOU ARE MY SON, AND I WON'T SEE YOU SUFFER.
RRGH! BETTER!
HEAR ME, ALL YOU GODS AND GODDESSES. LEAVE ME NOW!
GO NOT AMONGST THE TROJANS TO HELP THEM, OR THE GREEKS, UNLESS YOU WISH MY ANGER!

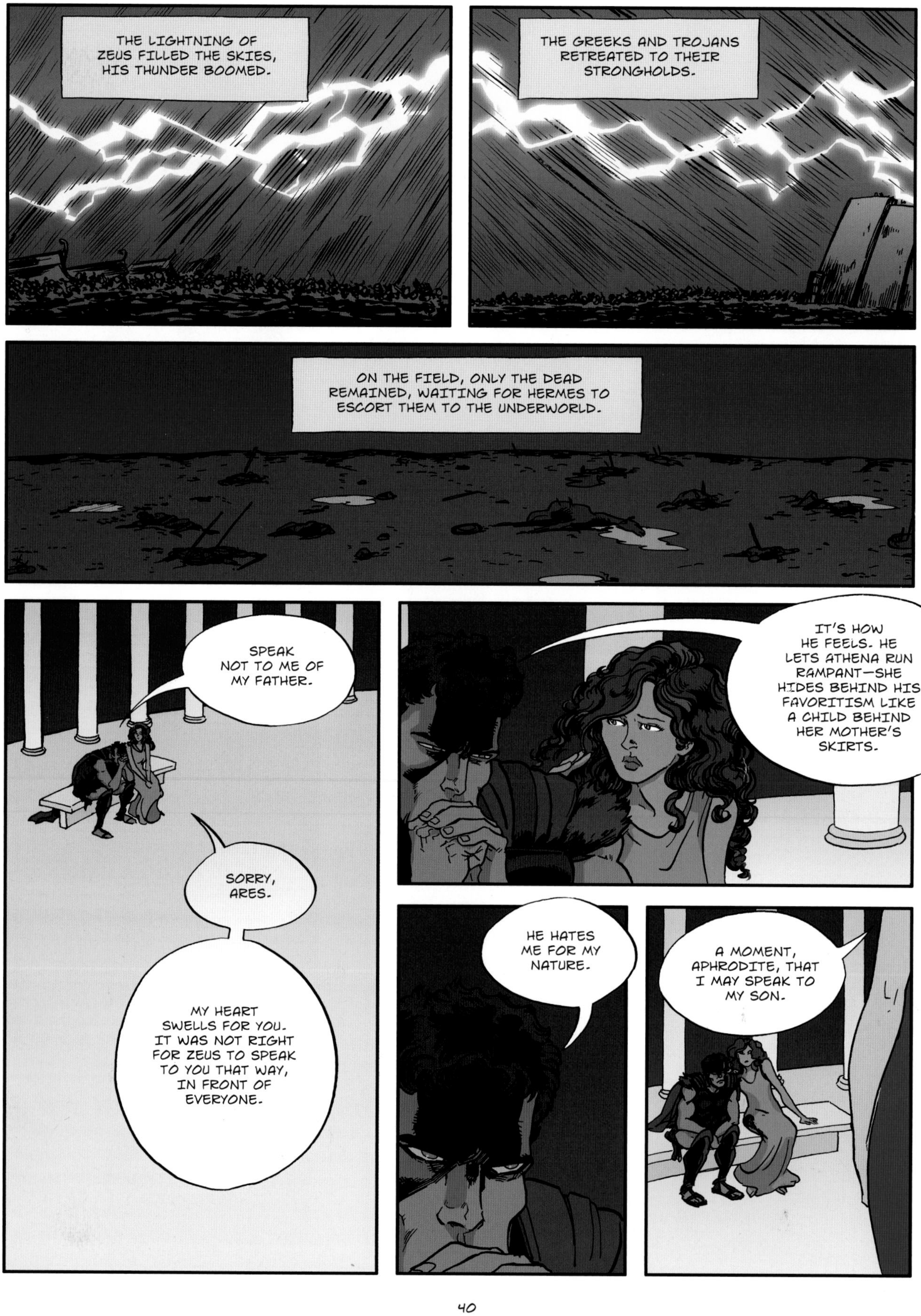
THE LIGHTNING OF ZEUS FILLED THE SKIES, HIS THUNDER BOOMED.
THE GREEKS AND TROJANS RETREATED TO THEIR STRONGHOLDS.
ON THE FIELD, ONLY THE DEAD REMAINED, WAITING FOR HERMES TO ESCORT THEM TO THE UNDERWORLD.
SPEAK NOT TO ME OF MY FATHER.
SORRY, ARES.
MY HEART SWELLS FOR YOU. IT WAS NOT RIGHT FOR ZEUS TO SPEAK TO YOU THAT WAY, IN FRONT OF EVERYONE.
IT'S HOW HE FEELS. HE LETS ATHENA RUN RAMPANT—SHE HIDES BEHIND HIS FAVORITISM LIKE A CHILD BEHIND HER MOTHER'S SKIRTS.
HE HATES ME FOR MY NATURE.
A MOMENT, APHRODITE, THAT I MAY SPEAK TO MY SON.

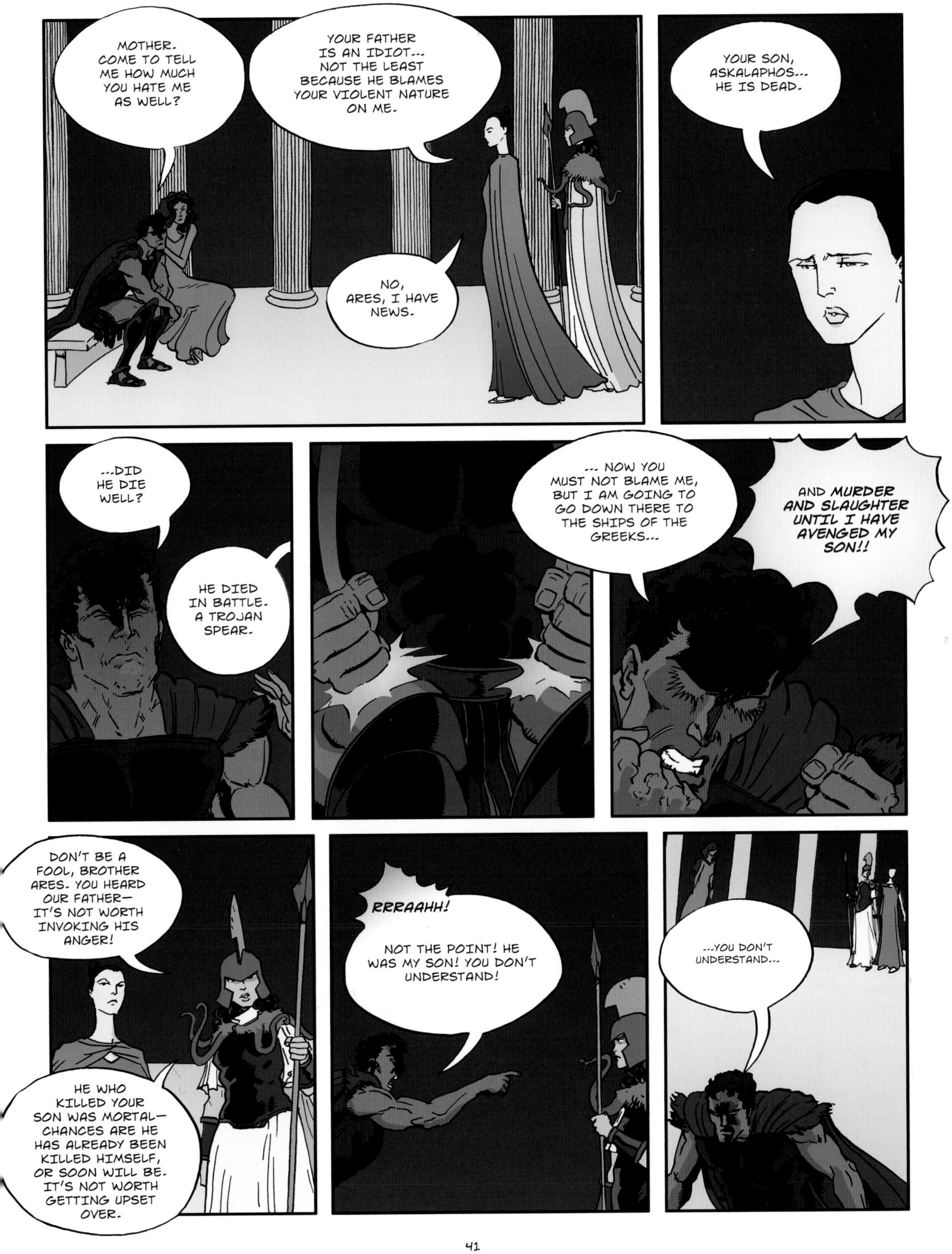
MOTHER. COME TO TELL ME HOW MUCH YOU HATE ME AS WELL?
YOUR FATHER IS AN IDIOT... NOT THE LEAST BECAUSE HE BLAMES YOUR VIOLENT NATURE ON ME.
NO, ARES, I HAVE NEWS.
YOUR SON, ASKALAPHOS... HE IS DEAD.
...DID HE DIE WELL?
HE DIED IN BATTLE. A TROJAN SPEAR.
... NOW YOU MUST NOT BLAME ME, BUT I AM GOING TO GO DOWN THERE TO THE SHIPS OF THE GREEKS...
AND MURDER AND SLAUGHTER UNTIL I HAVE AVENGED MY SON!!
DON'T BE A FOOL, BROTHER ARES. YOU HEARD OUR FATHER— IT'S NOT WORTH INVOKING HIS ANGER!
HE WHO KILLED YOUR SON WAS MORTAL— CHANCES ARE HE HAS ALREADY BEEN KILLED HIMSELF, OR SOON WILL BE. IT'S NOT WORTH GETTING UPSET OVER.
RRRAAHH!
NOT THE POINT! HE WAS MY SON! YOU DON'T UNDERSTAND!
...YOU DON'T UNDERSTAND...

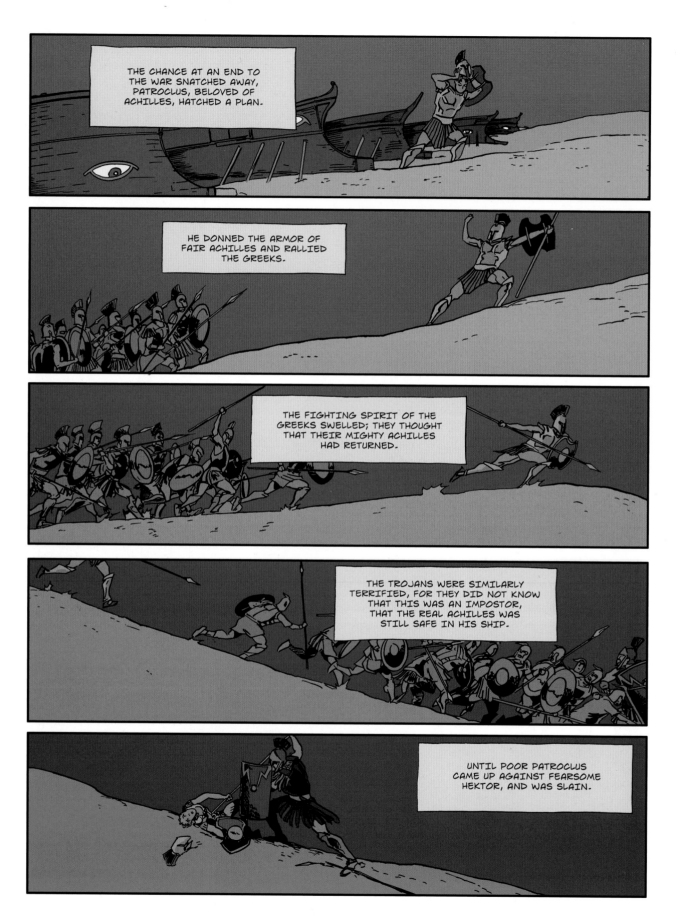

THE CHANCE AT AN END TO THE WAR SNATCHED AWAY, PATROCLUS, BELOVED OF ACHILLES, HATCHED A PLAN.

HE DONNED THE ARMOR OF FAIR ACHILLES AND RALLIED THE GREEKS.

THE FIGHTING SPIRIT OF THE GREEKS SWELLED; THEY THOUGHT THAT THEIR MIGHTY ACHILLES HAD RETURNED.

THE TROJANS WERE SIMILARLY TERRIFIED, FOR THEY DID NOT KNOW THAT THIS WAS AN IMPOSTOR, THAT THE REAL ACHILLES WAS STILL SAFE IN HIS SHIP.

UNTIL POOR PATROCLUS CAME UP AGAINST FEARSOME HEKTOR, AND WAS SLAIN.

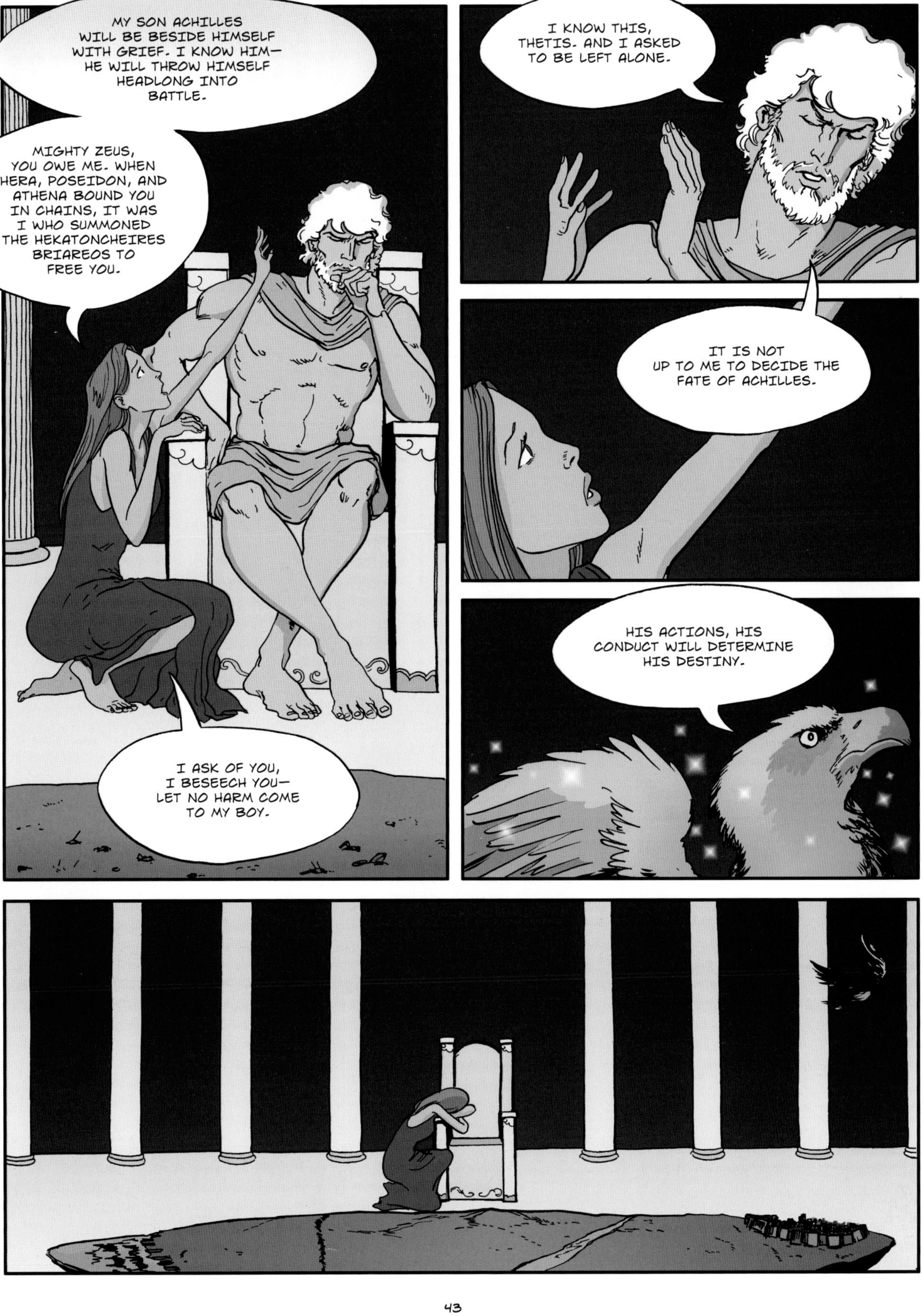
MY SON ACHILLES WILL BE BESIDE HIMSELF WITH GRIEF. I KNOW HIM— HE WILL THROW HIMSELF HEADLONG INTO BATTLE.
MIGHTY ZEUS, YOU OWE ME. WHEN HERA, POSEIDON, AND ATHENA BOUND YOU IN CHAINS, IT WAS I WHO SUMMONED THE HEKATONCHEIRES BRIAREOS TO FREE YOU.
I ASK OF YOU, I BESEECH YOU— LET NO HARM COME TO MY BOY.
I KNOW THIS, THETIS. AND I ASKED TO BE LEFT ALONE.
IT IS NOT UP TO ME TO DECIDE THE FATE OF ACHILLES.
HIS ACTIONS, HIS CONDUCT WILL DETERMINE HIS DESTINY.

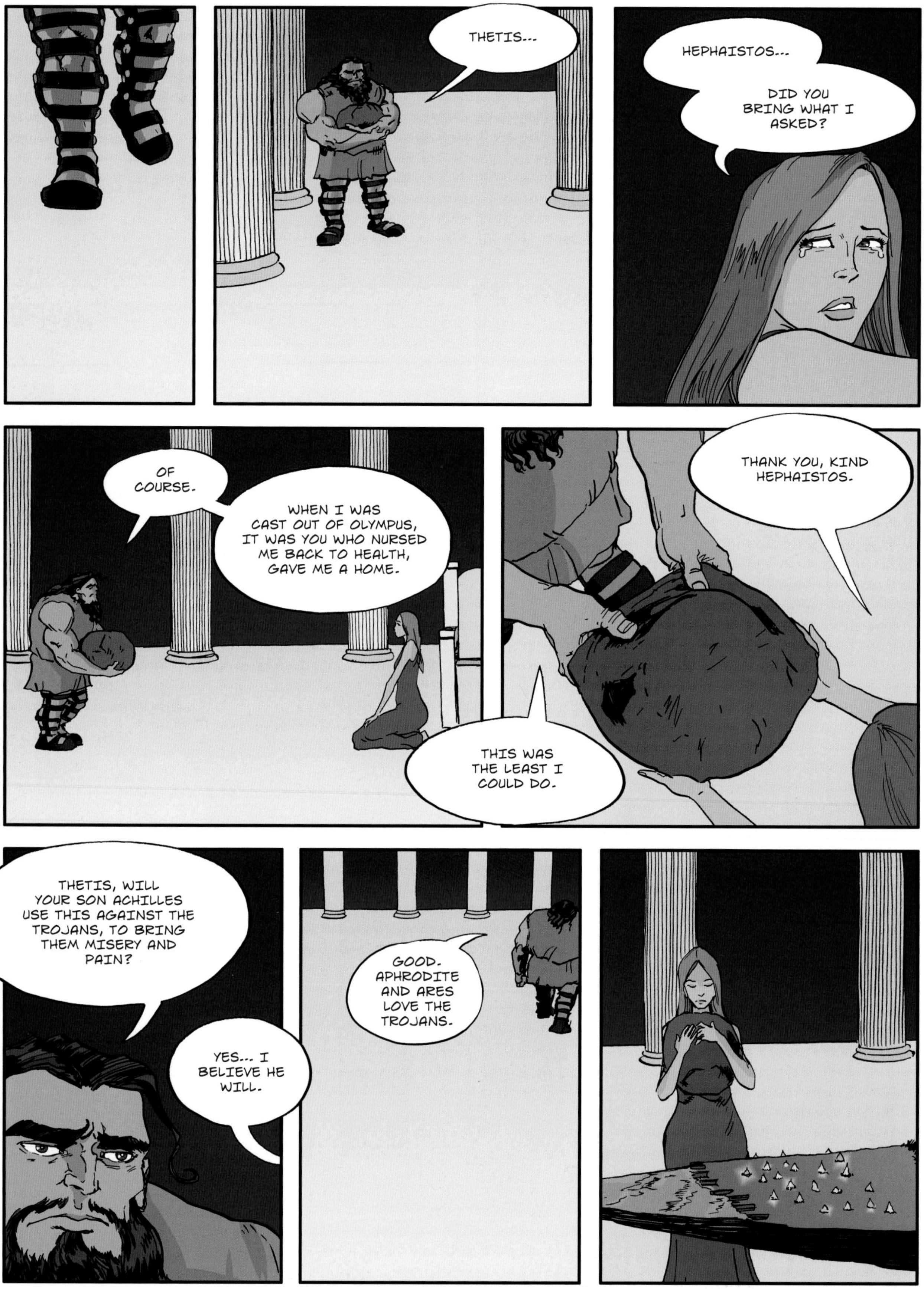
THETIS...
HEPHAISTOS...
DID YOU BRING WHAT I ASKED?
OF COURSE.
WHEN I WAS CAST OUT OF OLYMPUS, IT WAS YOU WHO NURSED ME BACK TO HEALTH, GAVE ME A HOME.
THANK YOU, KIND HEPHAISTOS.
THIS WAS THE LEAST I COULD DO.
THETIS, WILL YOUR SON ACHILLES USE THIS AGAINST THE TROJANS, TO BRING THEM MISERY AND PAIN?
YES... I BELIEVE HE WILL.
GOOD. APHRODITE AND ARES LOVE THE TROJANS.

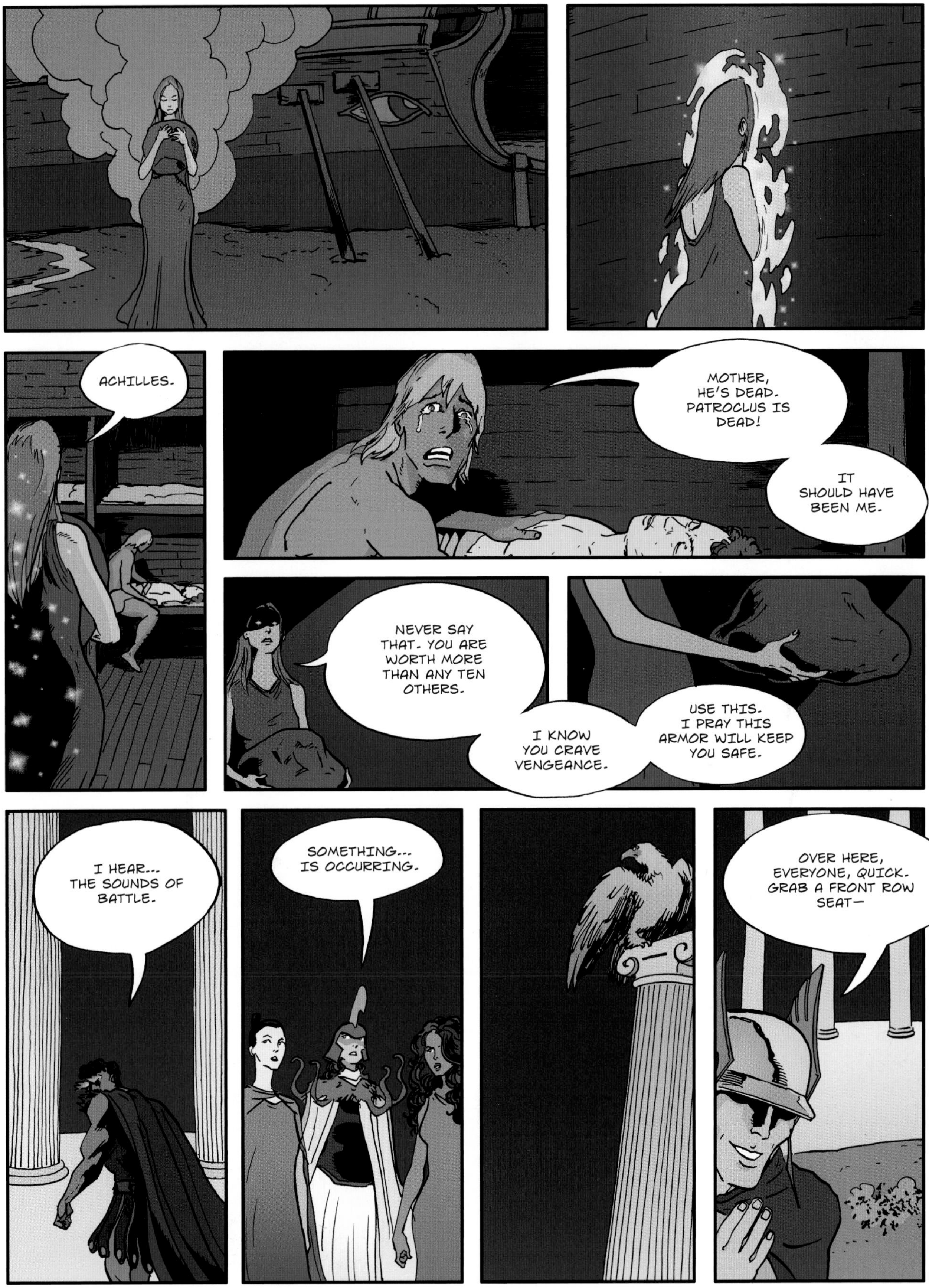
ACHILLES.
MOTHER, HE'S DEAD. PATROCLUS IS DEAD!
IT SHOULD HAVE BEEN ME.
NEVER SAY THAT. YOU ARE WORTH MORE THAN ANY TEN OTHERS.
I KNOW YOU CRAVE VENGEANCE.
USE THIS. I PRAY THIS ARMOR WILL KEEP YOU SAFE.
I HEAR... THE SOUNDS OF BATTLE.
SOMETHING... IS OCCURRING.
OVER HERE, EVERYONE, QUICK. GRAB A FRONT ROW SEAT—

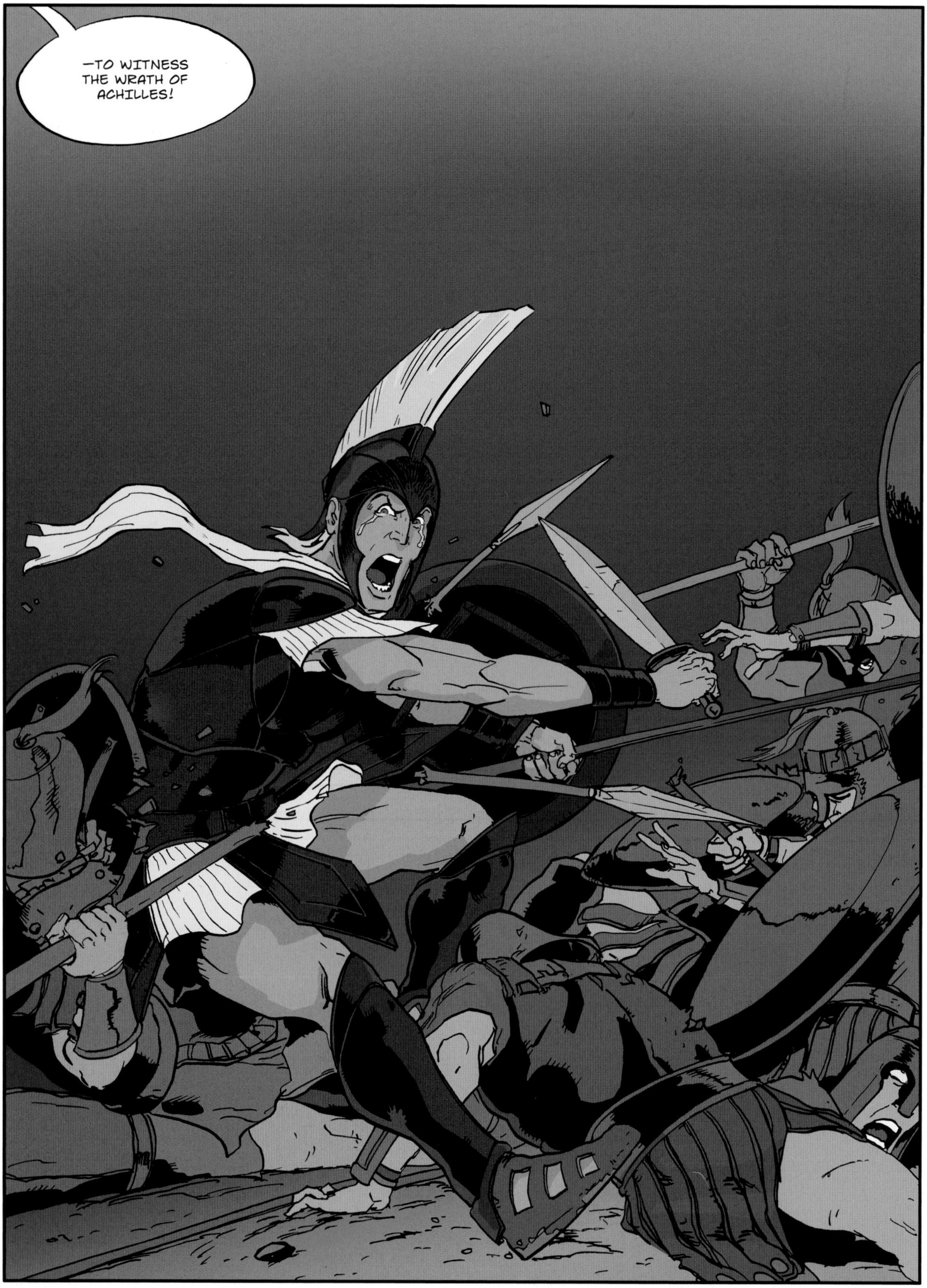
—TO WITNESS THE WRATH OF ACHILLES!

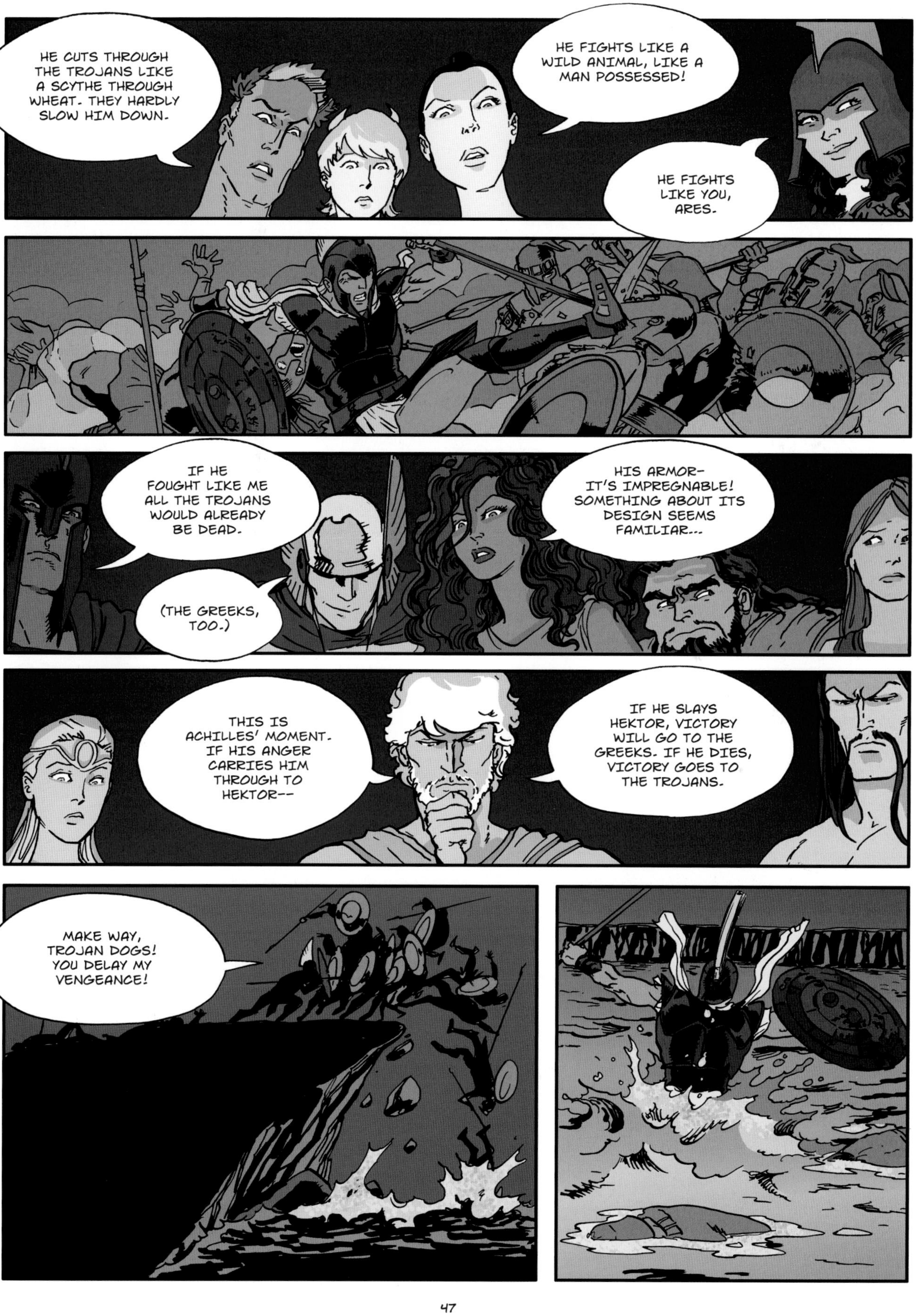
HE CUTS THROUGH THE TROJANS LIKE A SCYTHE THROUGH WHEAT. THEY HARDLY SLOW HIM DOWN.
HE FIGHTS LIKE A WILD ANIMAL, LIKE A MAN POSSESSED!
HE FIGHTS LIKE YOU, ARES.
IF HE FOUGHT LIKE ME ALL THE TROJANS WOULD ALREADY BE DEAD.
(THE GREEKS, TOO.)
HIS ARMOR— IT'S IMPREGNABLE! SOMETHING ABOUT ITS DESIGN SEEMS FAMILIAR...
THIS IS ACHILLES' MOMENT. IF HIS ANGER CARRIES HIM THROUGH TO HEKTOR--
IF HE SLAYS HEKTOR, VICTORY WILL GO TO THE GREEKS. IF HE DIES, VICTORY GOES TO THE TROJANS.
MAKE WAY, TROJAN DOGS! YOU DELAY MY VENGEANCE!

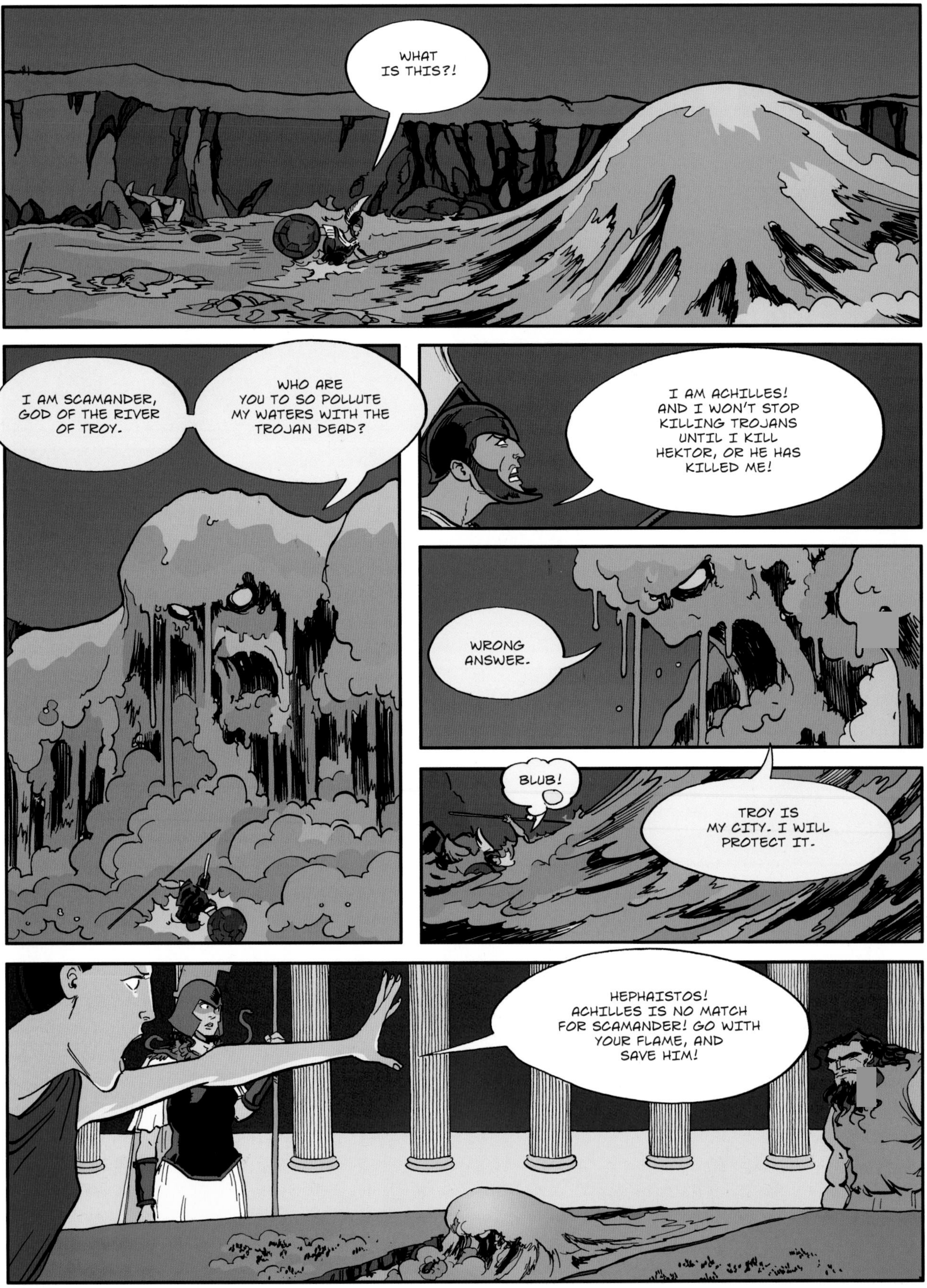
WHAT IS THIS?!
I AM SCAMANDER, GOD OF THE RIVER OF TROY.
WHO ARE YOU TO SO POLLUTE MY WATERS WITH THE TROJAN DEAD?
I AM ACHILLES! AND I WON'T STOP KILLING TROJANS UNTIL I KILL HEKTOR, OR HE HAS KILLED ME!
WRONG ANSWER.
BLUB!
TROY IS MY CITY. I WILL PROTECT IT.
HEPHAISTOS! ACHILLES IS NO MATCH FOR SCAMANDER! GO WITH YOUR FLAME, AND SAVE HIM!

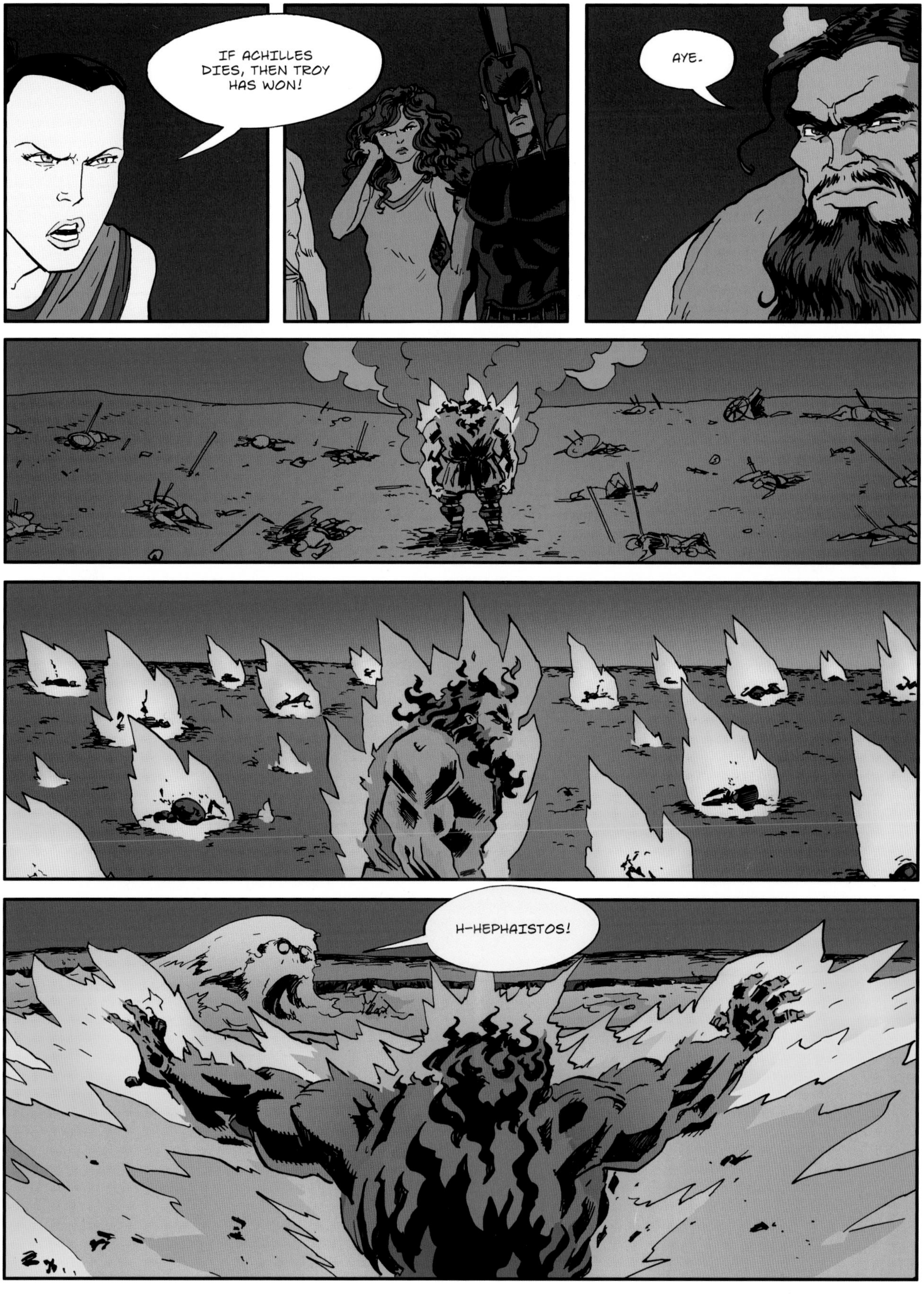
IF ACHILLES DIES, THEN TROY HAS WON!
AYE.
H-HEPHAISTOS!

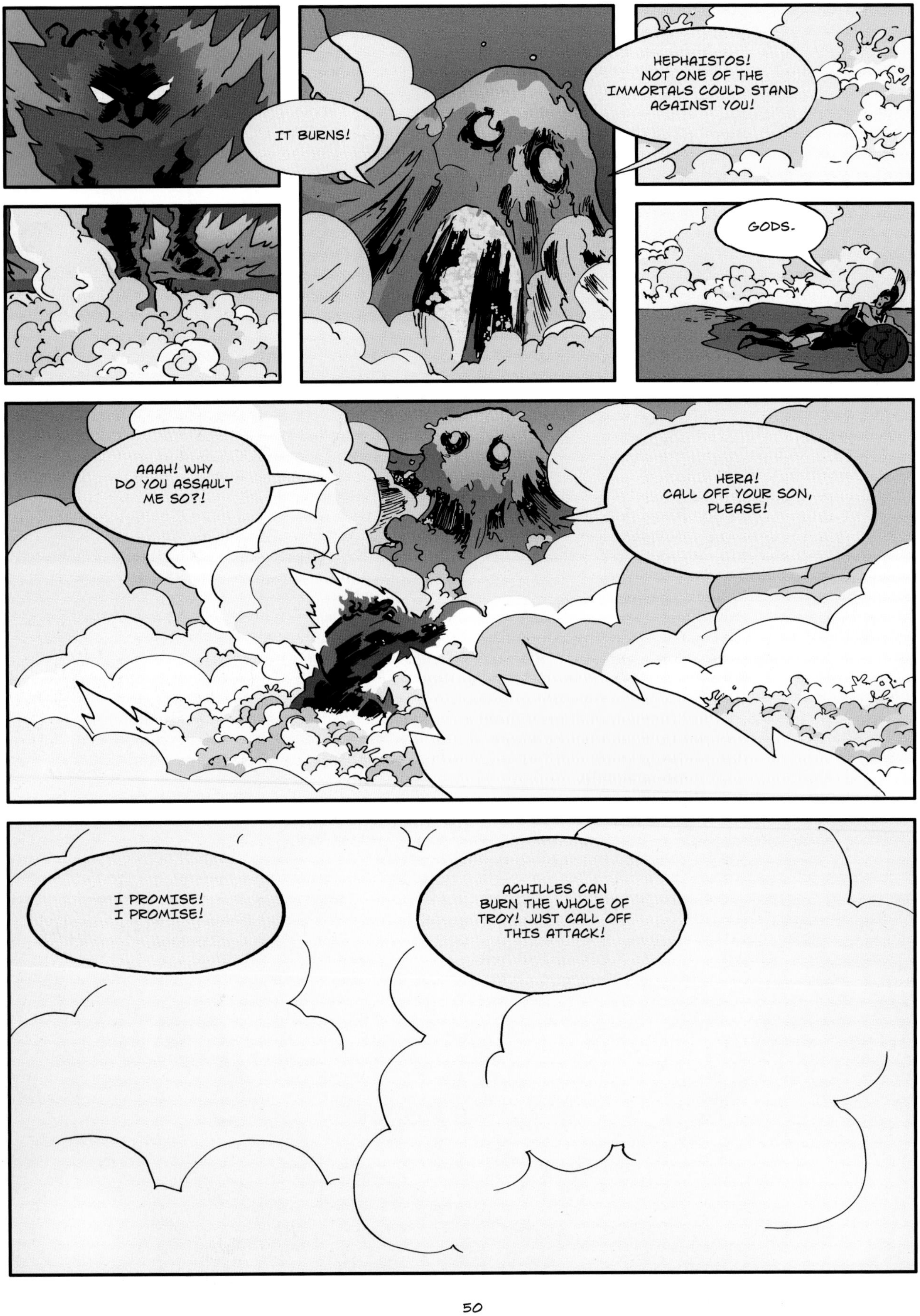
IT BURNS!
HEPHAISTOS! NOT ONE OF THE IMMORTALS COULD STAND AGAINST YOU!
GODS.
AAAH! WHY DO YOU ASSAULT ME SO?!
HERA! CALL OFF YOUR SON, PLEASE!
I PROMISE! I PROMISE!
ACHILLES CAN BURN THE WHOLE OF TROY! JUST CALL OFF THIS ATTACK!

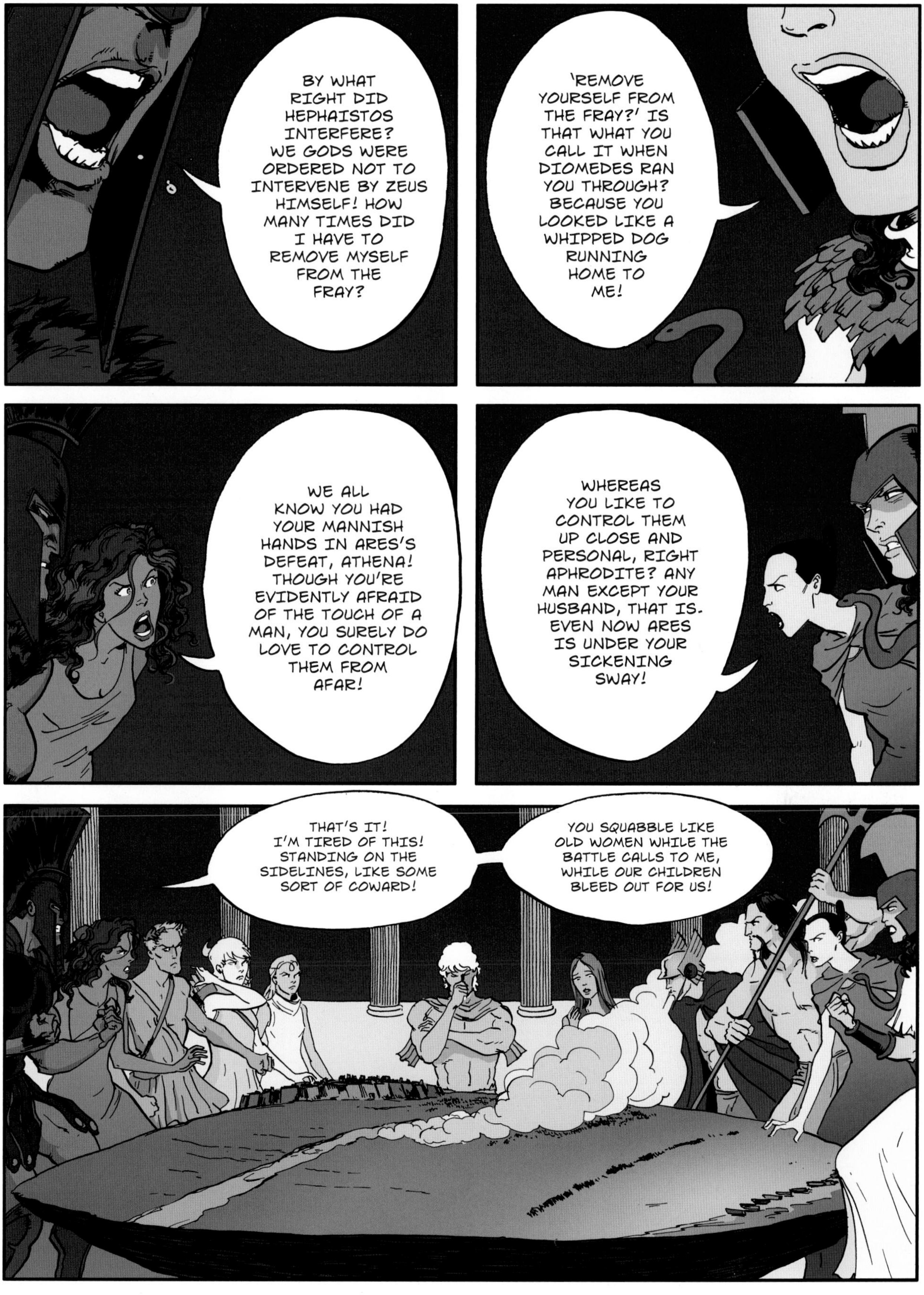
BY WHAT RIGHT DID HEPHAISTOS INTERFERE? WE GODS WERE ORDERED NOT TO INTERVENE BY ZEUS HIMSELF! HOW MANY TIMES DID I HAVE TO REMOVE MYSELF FROM THE FRAY?
'REMOVE YOURSELF FROM THE FRAY?' IS THAT WHAT YOU CALL IT WHEN DIOMEDES RAN YOU THROUGH? BECAUSE YOU LOOKED LIKE A WHIPPED DOG RUNNING HOME TO ME!
WE ALL KNOW YOU HAD YOUR MANNISH HANDS IN ARES'S DEFEAT, ATHENA! THOUGH YOU'RE EVIDENTLY AFRAID OF THE TOUCH OF A MAN, YOU SURELY DO LOVE TO CONTROL THEM FROM AFAR!
WHEREAS YOU LIKE TO CONTROL THEM UP CLOSE AND PERSONAL, RIGHT APHRODITE? ANY MAN EXCEPT YOUR HUSBAND, THAT IS. EVEN NOW ARES IS UNDER YOUR SICKENING SWAY!
THAT'S IT! I'M TIRED OF THIS! STANDING ON THE SIDELINES, LIKE SOME SORT OF COWARD!
YOU SQUABBLE LIKE OLD WOMEN WHILE THE BATTLE CALLS TO ME, WHILE OUR CHILDREN BLEED OUT FOR US!

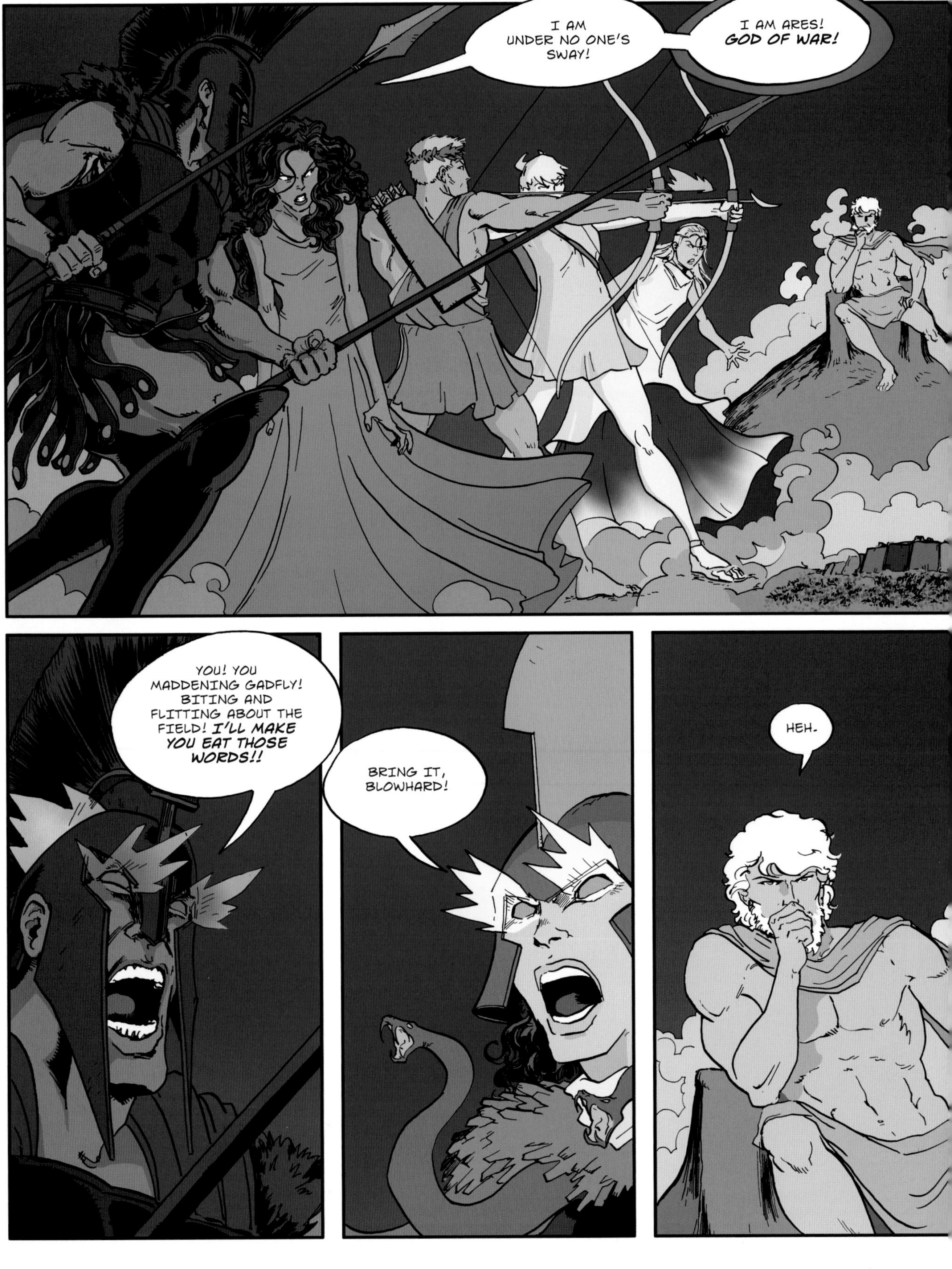
I AM UNDER NO ONE'S SWAY!
I AM ARES! GOD OF WAR!
YOU! YOU MADDENING GADFLY! BITING AND FLITTING ABOUT THE FIELD! I'LL MAKE YOU EAT THOSE WORDS!!
BRING IT, BLOWHARD!
HEH.

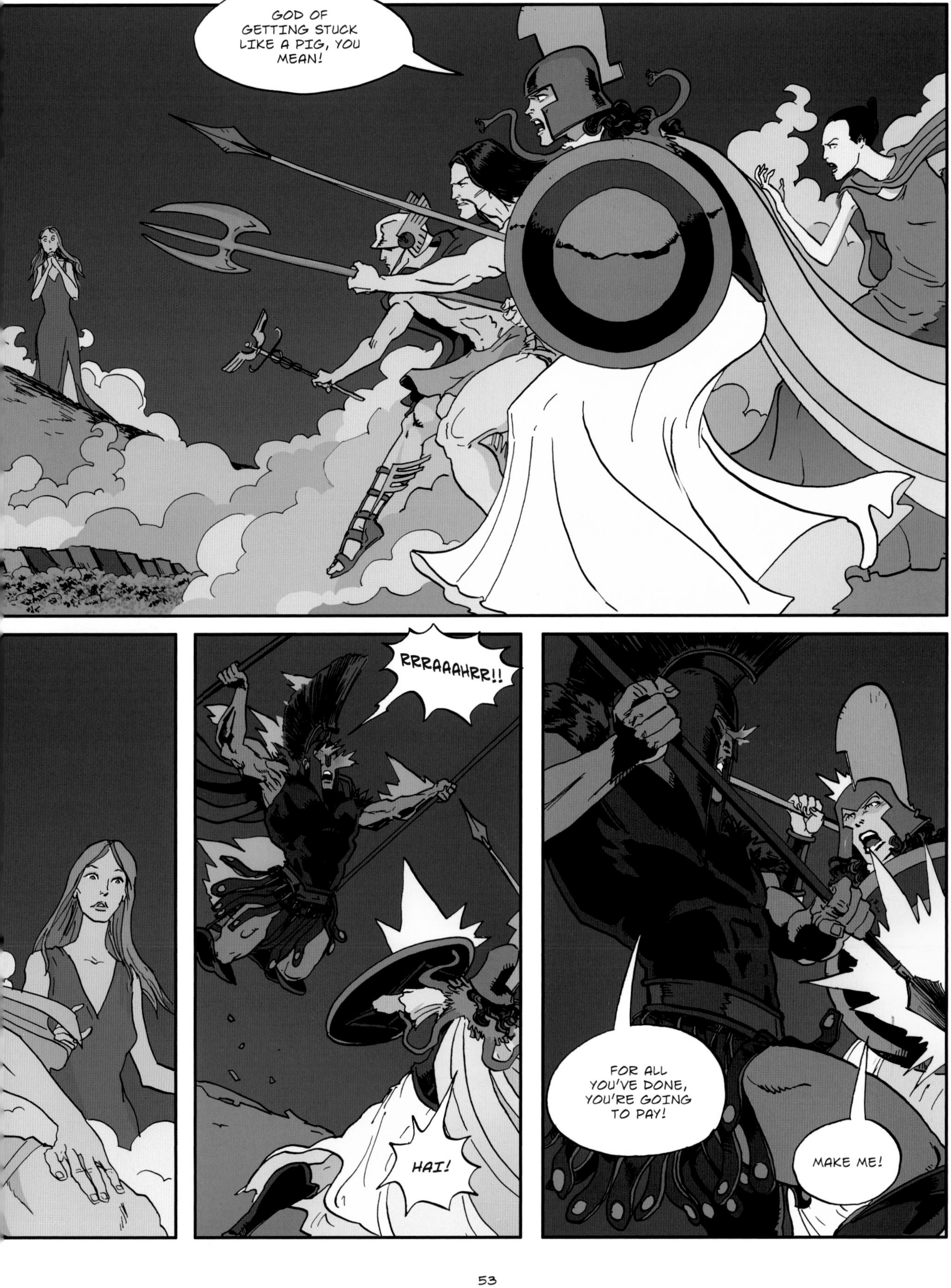
GOD OF GETTING STUCK LIKE A PIG, YOU MEAN!
RRRAAAHRR!!
HAI!
FOR ALL YOU'VE DONE, YOU'RE GOING TO PAY!
MAKE ME!

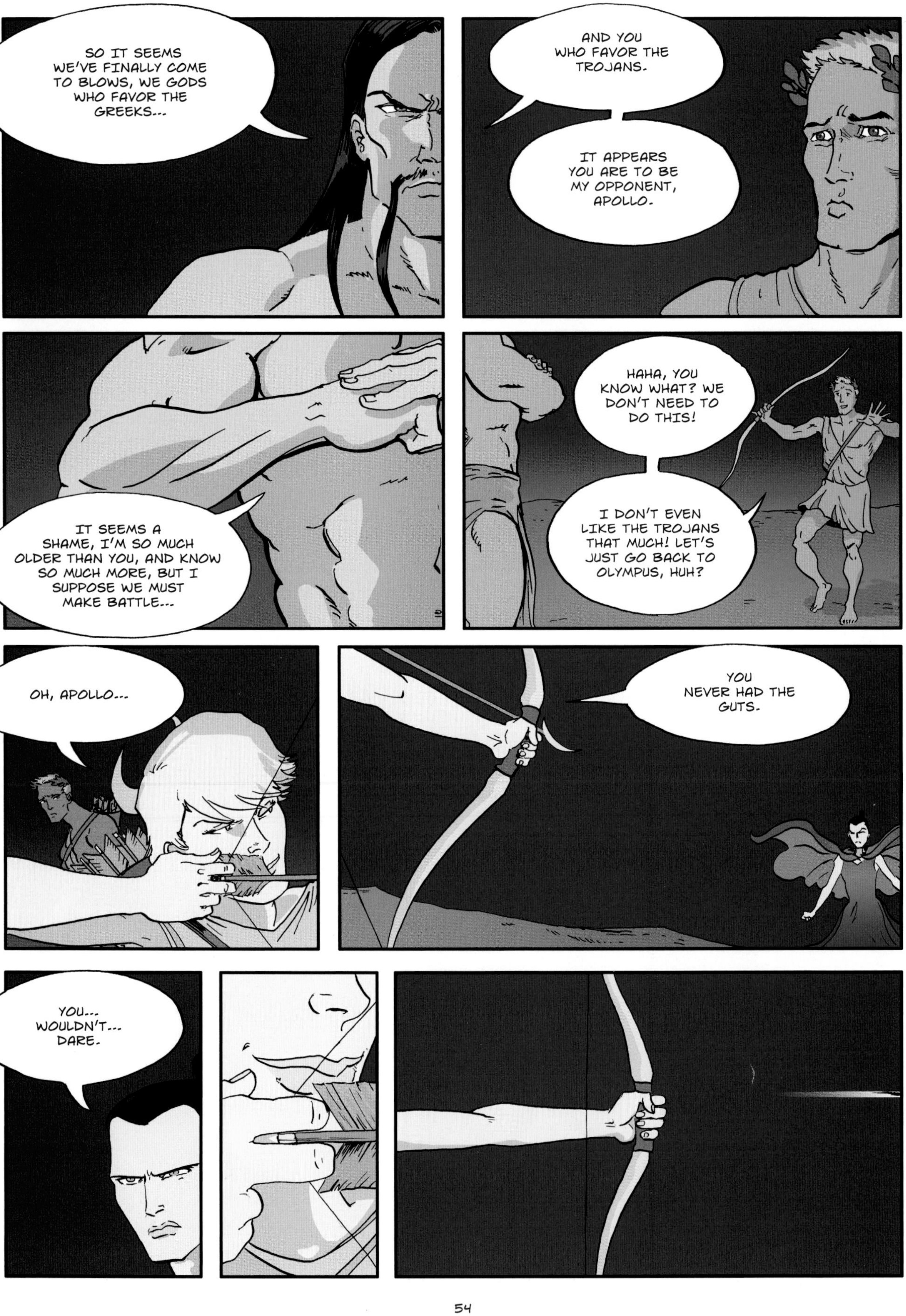
SO IT SEEMS WE'VE FINALLY COME TO BLOWS, WE GODS WHO FAVOR THE GREEKS...
AND YOU WHO FAVOR THE TROJANS.
IT APPEARS YOU ARE TO BE MY OPPONENT, APOLLO.
IT SEEMS A SHAME, I'M SO MUCH OLDER THAN YOU, AND KNOW SO MUCH MORE, BUT I SUPPOSE WE MUST MAKE BATTLE...
HAHA, YOU KNOW WHAT? WE DON'T NEED TO DO THIS!
I DON'T EVEN LIKE THE TROJANS THAT MUCH! LET'S JUST GO BACK TO OLYMPUS, HUH?
OH, APOLLO...
YOU NEVER HAD THE GUTS.
YOU... WOULDN'T... DARE.

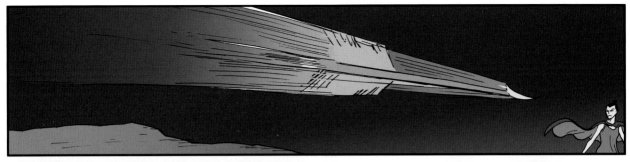

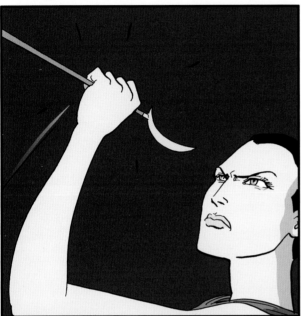

UH-OH.

UH—

YOU THOUGHT YOU WERE A MATCH FOR ME?

STICK TO HUNTING DEER.

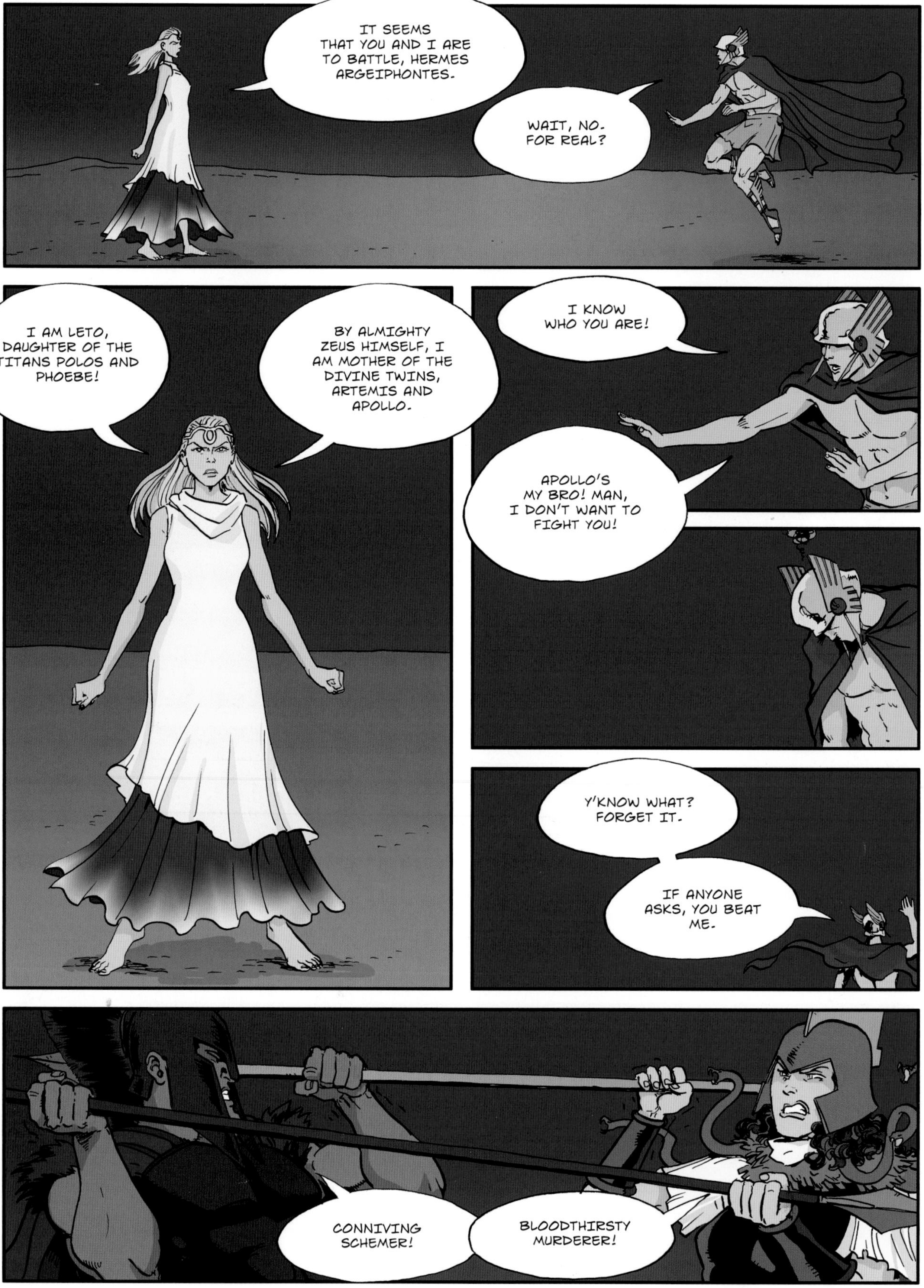
IT SEEMS THAT YOU AND I ARE TO BATTLE, HERMES ARGEIPHONTES.
WAIT, NO. FOR REAL?
I AM LETO, DAUGHTER OF THE TITANS POLOS AND PHOEBE!
BY ALMIGHTY ZEUS HIMSELF, I AM MOTHER OF THE DIVINE TWINS, ARTEMIS AND APOLLO.
I KNOW WHO YOU ARE!
APOLLO'S MY BRO! MAN, I DON'T WANT TO FIGHT YOU!
Y'KNOW WHAT? FORGET IT.
IF ANYONE ASKS, YOU BEAT ME.
CONNIVING SCHEMER!
BLOODTHIRSTY MURDERER!

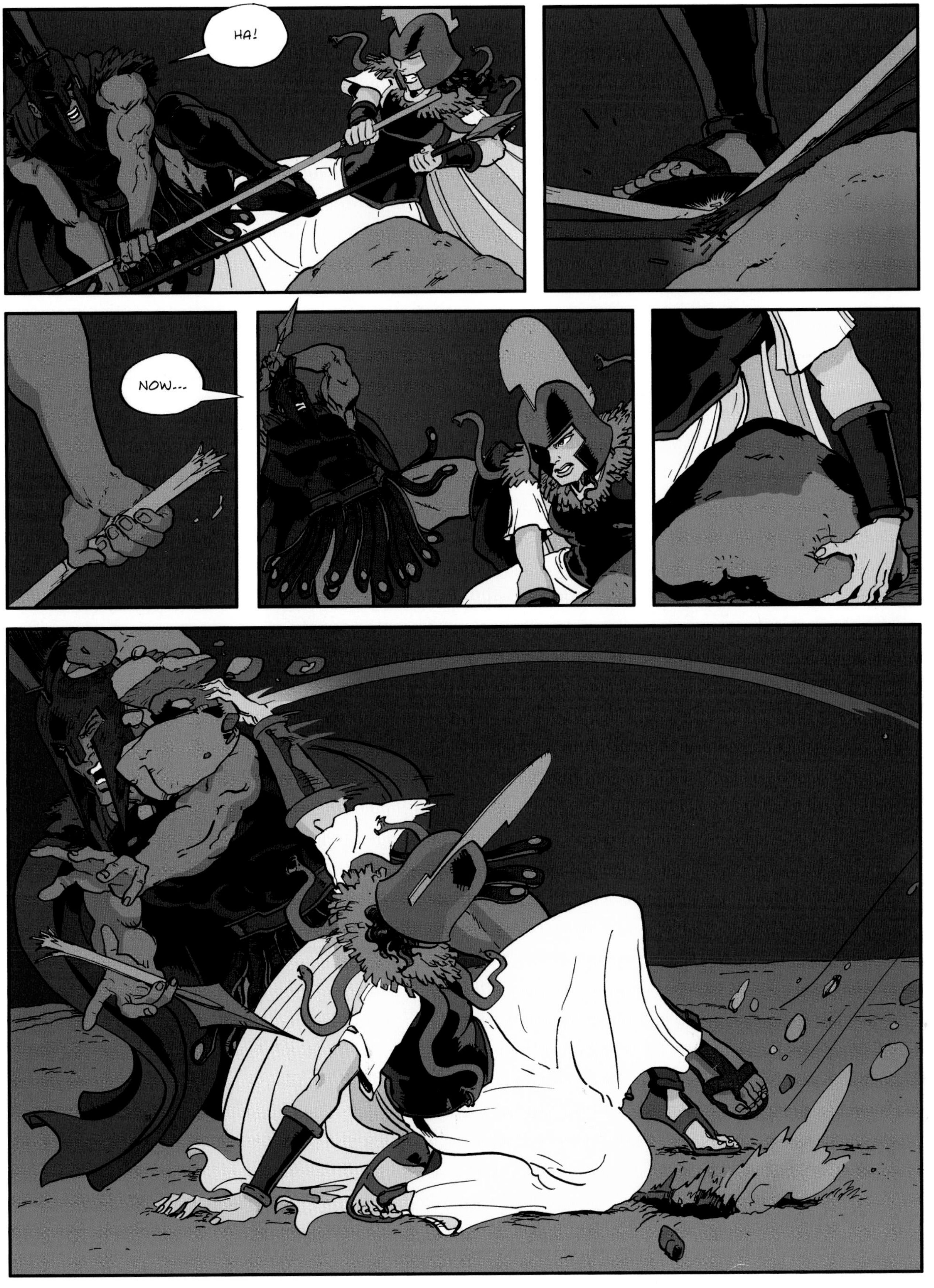
HA!
NOW...

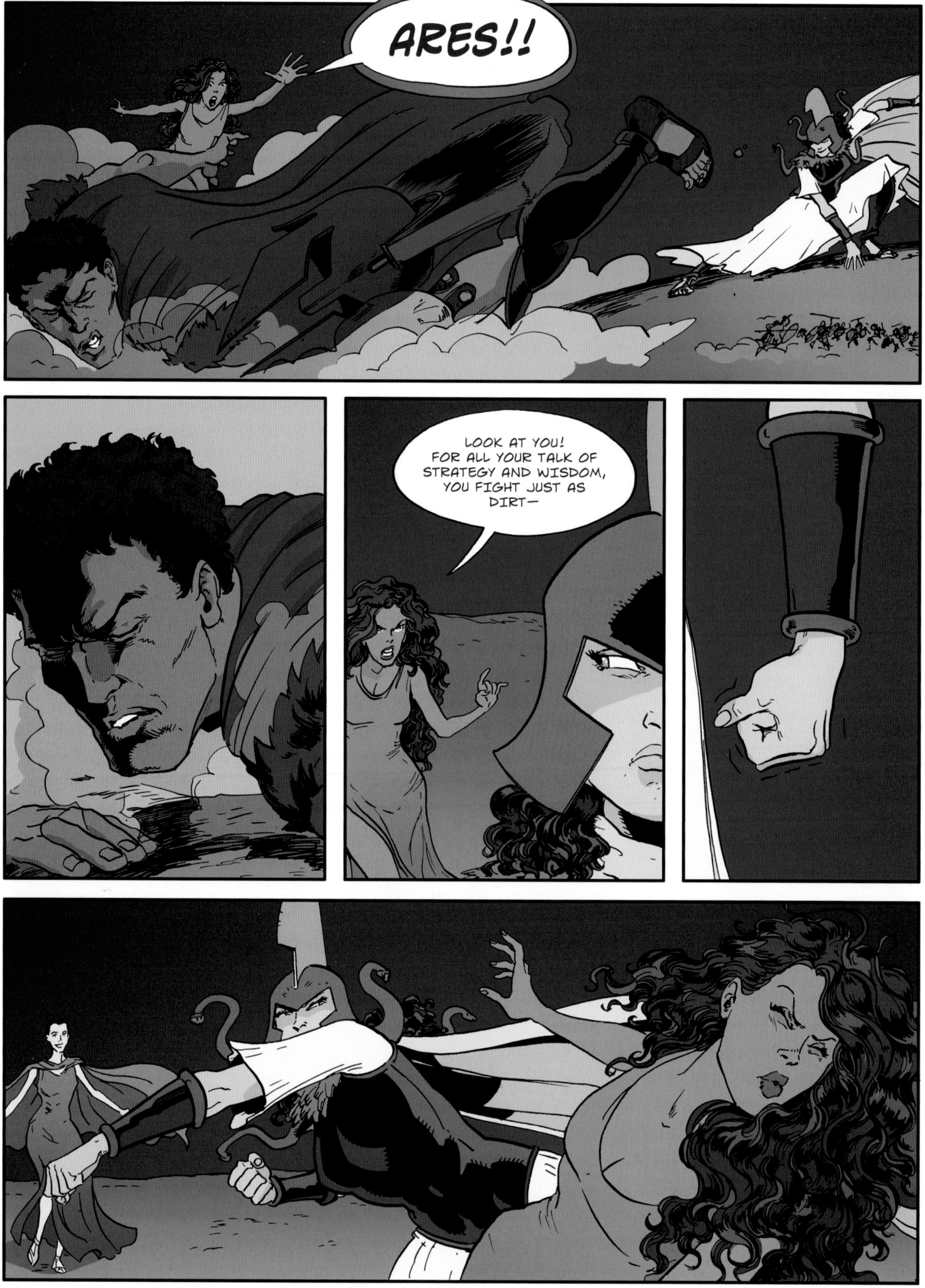
ARES!!
LOOK AT YOU! FOR ALL YOUR TALK OF STRATEGY AND WISDOM, YOU FIGHT JUST AS DIRT—

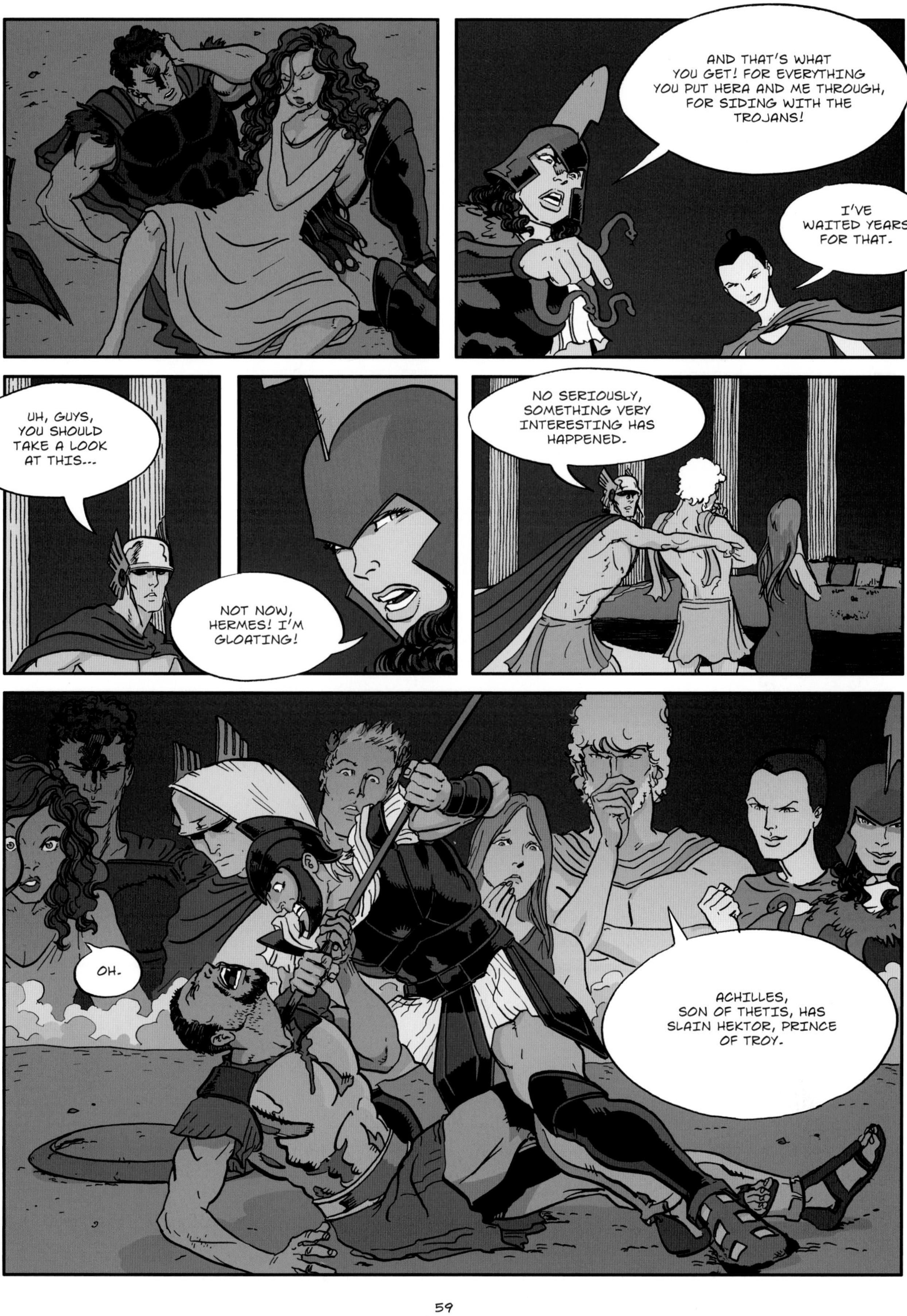
AND THAT'S WHAT YOU GET! FOR EVERYTHING YOU PUT HERA AND ME THROUGH, FOR SIDING WITH THE TROJANS!
I'VE WAITED YEARS FOR THAT.
UH, GUYS, YOU SHOULD TAKE A LOOK AT THIS...
NOT NOW, HERMES! I'M GLOATING!
NO SERIOUSLY, SOMETHING VERY INTERESTING HAS HAPPENED.
OH.
ACHILLES, SON OF THETIS, HAS SLAIN HEKTOR, PRINCE OF TROY.

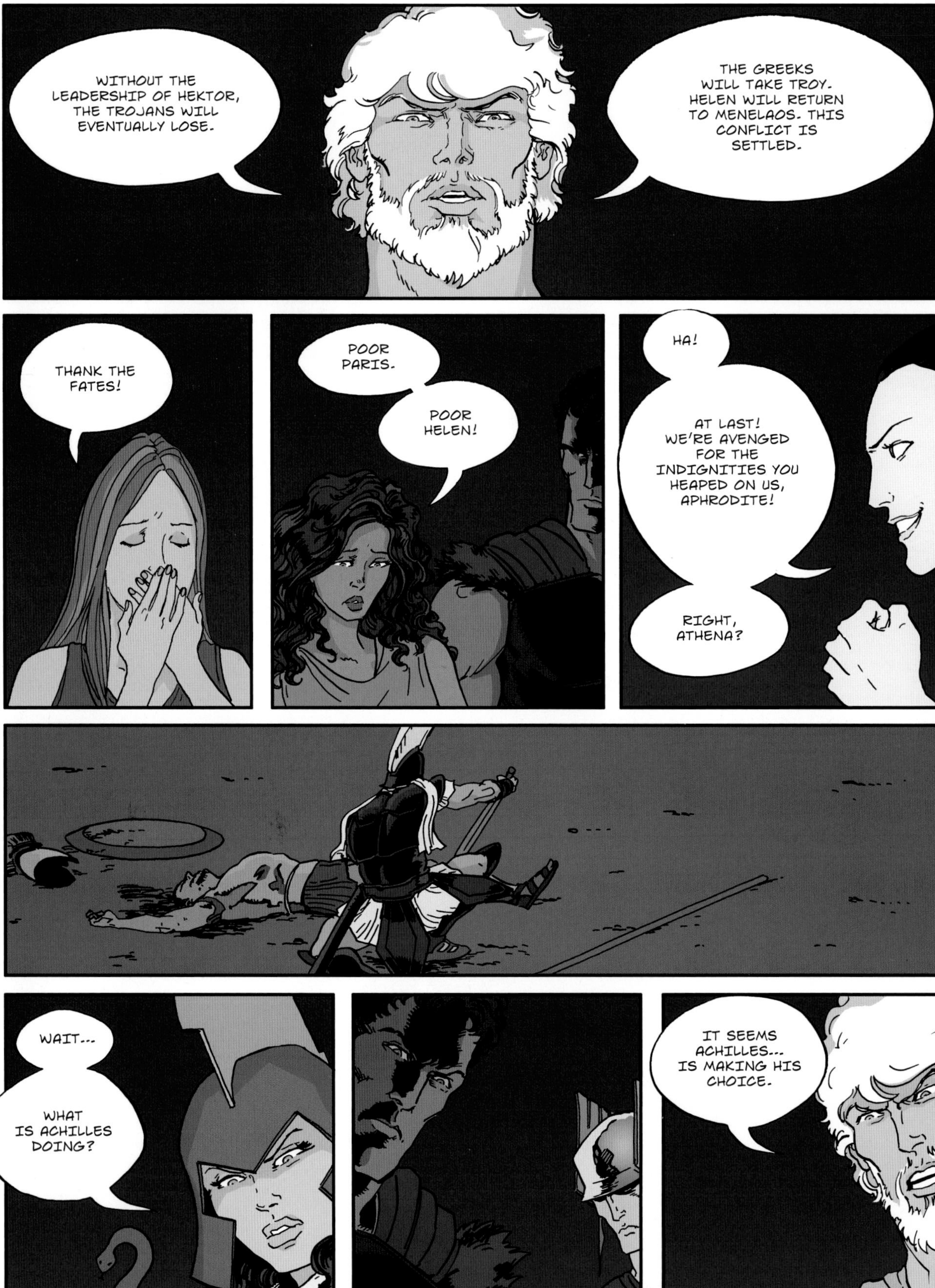
WITHOUT THE LEADERSHIP OF HEKTOR, THE TROJANS WILL EVENTUALLY LOSE.
THE GREEKS WILL TAKE TROY. HELEN WILL RETURN TO MENELAOS. THIS CONFLICT IS SETTLED.
THANK THE FATES!
POOR PARIS.
POOR HELEN!
HA!
AT LAST! WE'RE AVENGED FOR THE INDIGNITIES YOU HEAPED ON US, APHRODITE!
RIGHT, ATHENA?
WAIT...
WHAT IS ACHILLES DOING?
IT SEEMS ACHILLES... IS MAKING HIS CHOICE.

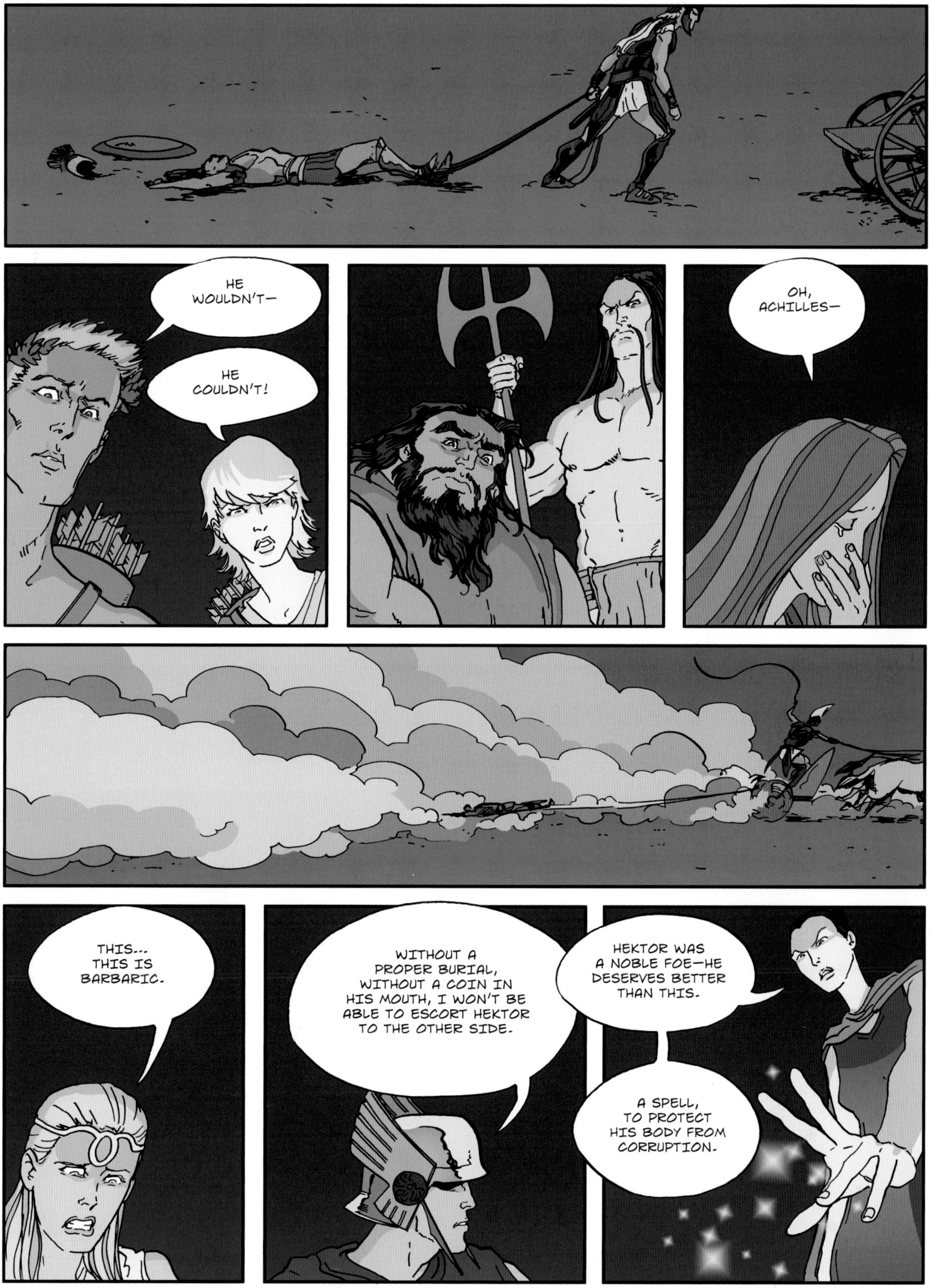
HE WOULDN'T—
HE COULDN'T!
OH, ACHILLES—
THIS... THIS IS BARBARIC.
WITHOUT A PROPER BURIAL, WITHOUT A COIN IN HIS MOUTH, I WON'T BE ABLE TO ESCORT HEKTOR TO THE OTHER SIDE.
HEKTOR WAS A NOBLE FOE—HE DESERVES BETTER THAN THIS.
A SPELL, TO PROTECT HIS BODY FROM CORRUPTION.

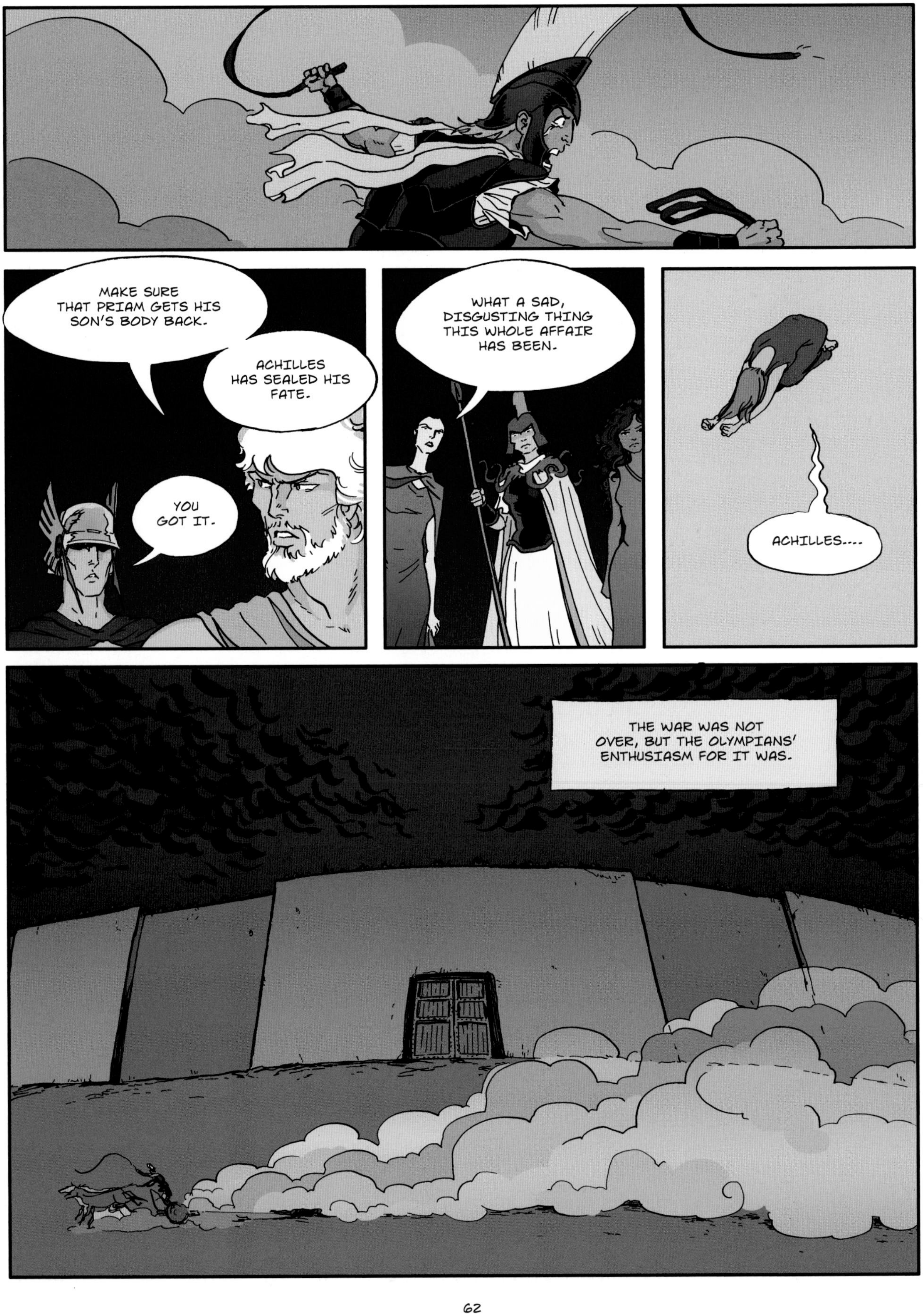
MAKE SURE THAT PRIAM GETS HIS SON'S BODY BACK.
ACHILLES HAS SEALED HIS FATE.
YOU GOT IT.
WHAT A SAD, DISGUSTING THING THIS WHOLE AFFAIR HAS BEEN.
ACHILLES....
THE WAR WAS NOT OVER, BUT THE OLYMPIANS' ENTHUSIASM FOR IT WAS.

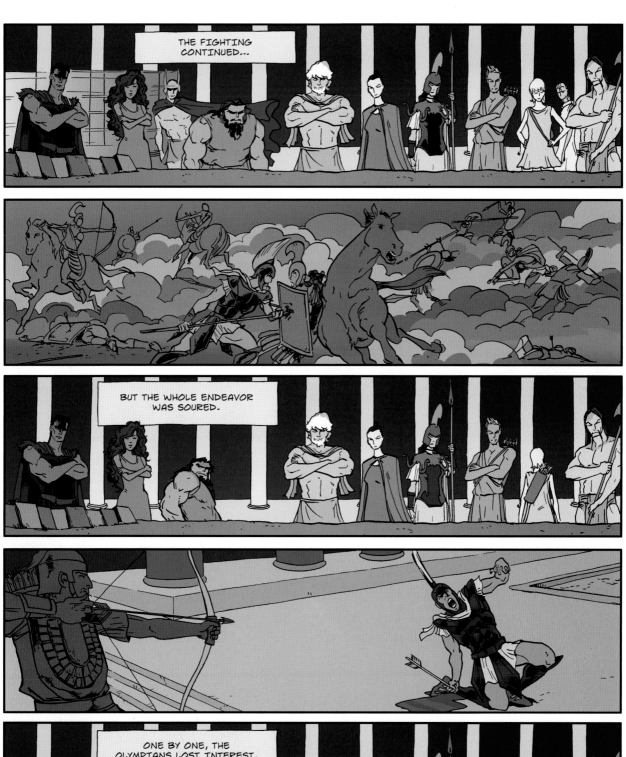

THE FIGHTING
CONTINUED...

BUT THE WHOLE ENDEAVOR
WAS SOURED.

ONE BY ONE, THE
OLYMPIANS LOST INTEREST.

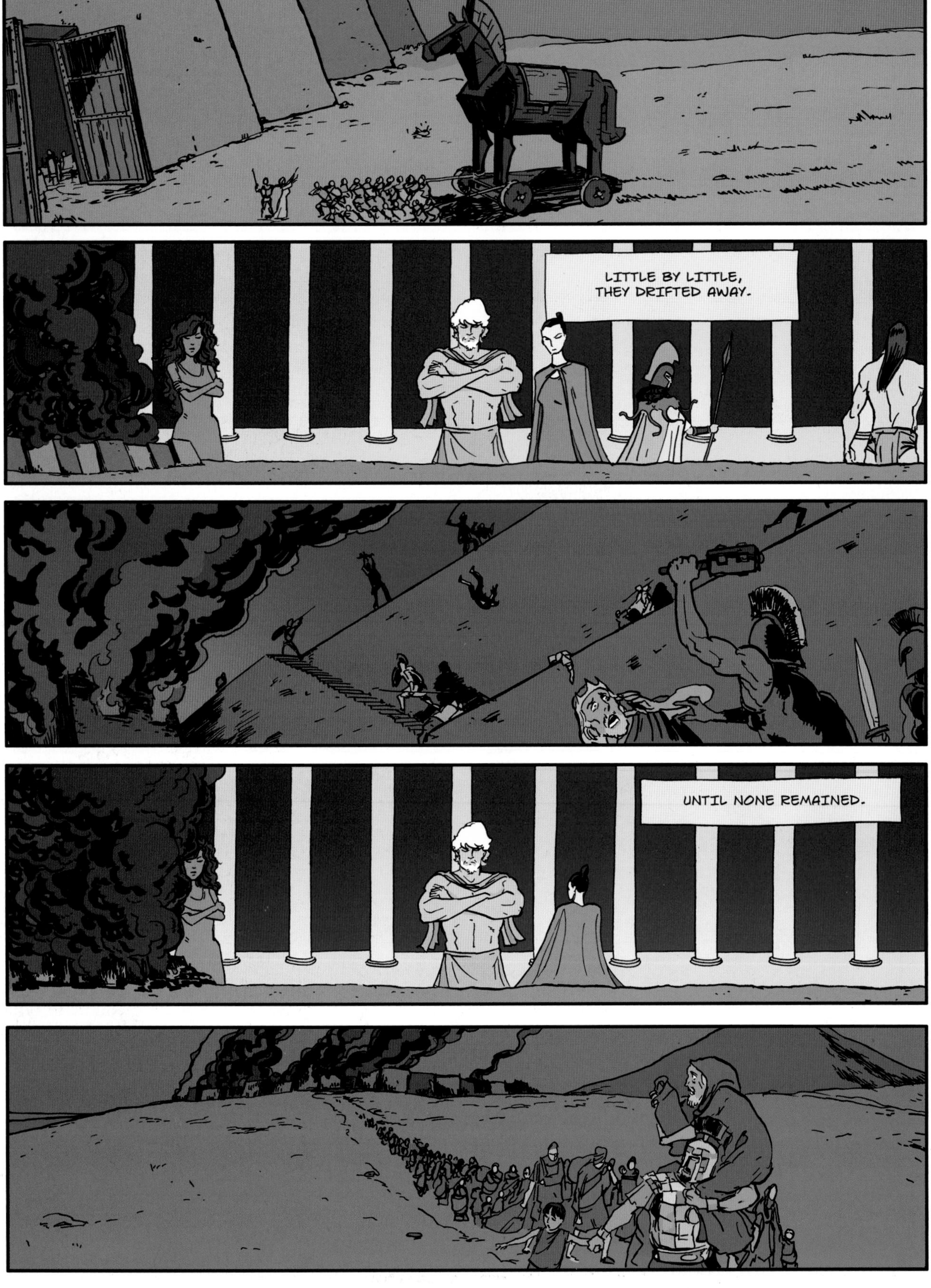
LITTLE BY LITTLE, THEY DRIFTED AWAY.
UNTIL NONE REMAINED.

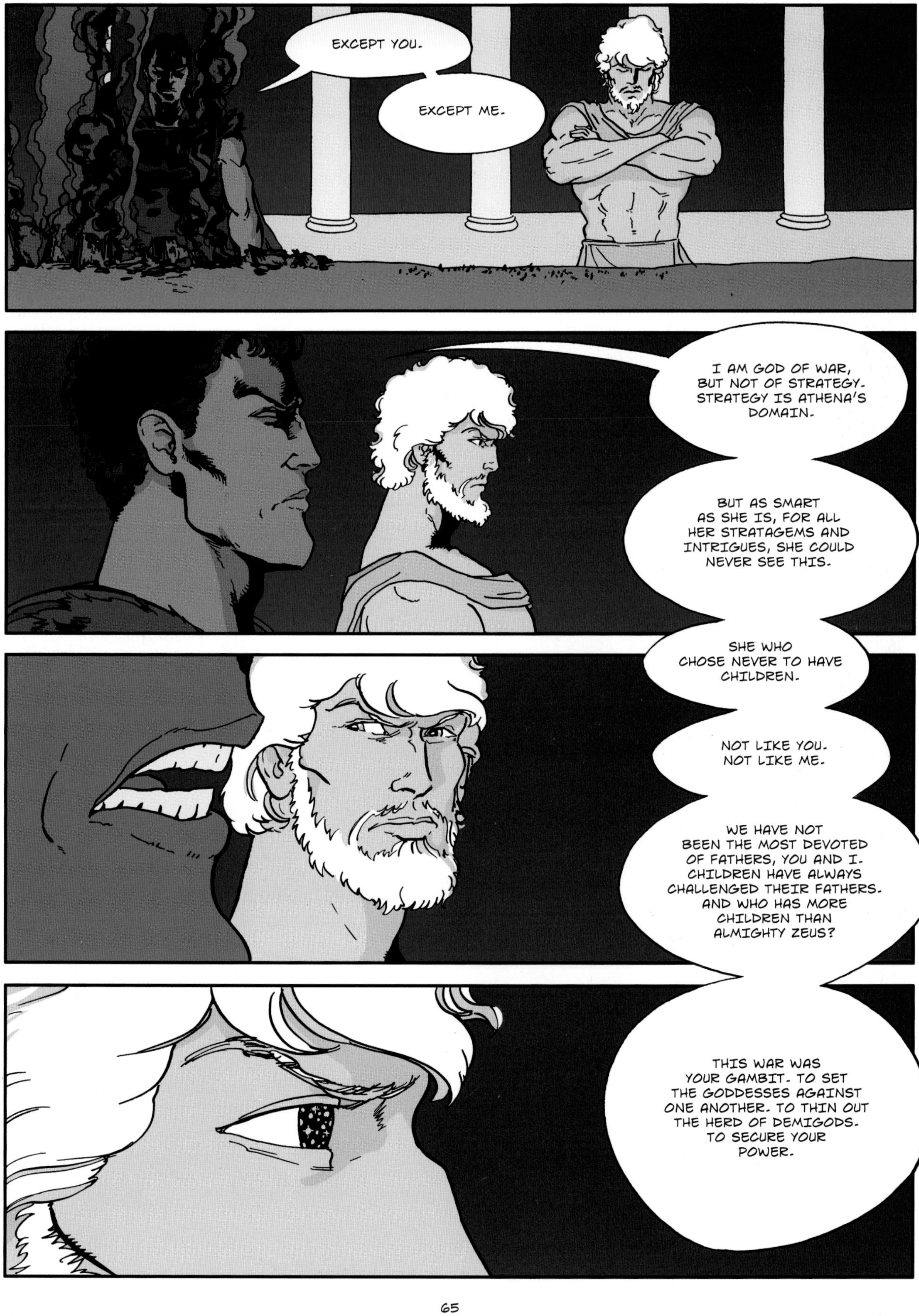
EXCEPT YOU.
EXCEPT ME.
I AM GOD OF WAR, BUT NOT OF STRATEGY. STRATEGY IS ATHENA'S DOMAIN.
BUT AS SMART AS SHE IS, FOR ALL HER STRATAGEMS AND INTRIGUES, SHE COULD NEVER SEE THIS.
SHE WHO CHOSE NEVER TO HAVE CHILDREN.
NOT LIKE YOU. NOT LIKE ME.
WE HAVE NOT BEEN THE MOST DEVOTED OF FATHERS, YOU AND I. CHILDREN HAVE ALWAYS CHALLENGED THEIR FATHERS. AND WHO HAS MORE CHILDREN THAN ALMIGHTY ZEUS?
THIS WAR WAS YOUR GAMBIT. TO SET THE GODDESSES AGAINST ONE ANOTHER. TO THIN OUT THE HERD OF DEMIGODS. TO SECURE YOUR POWER.

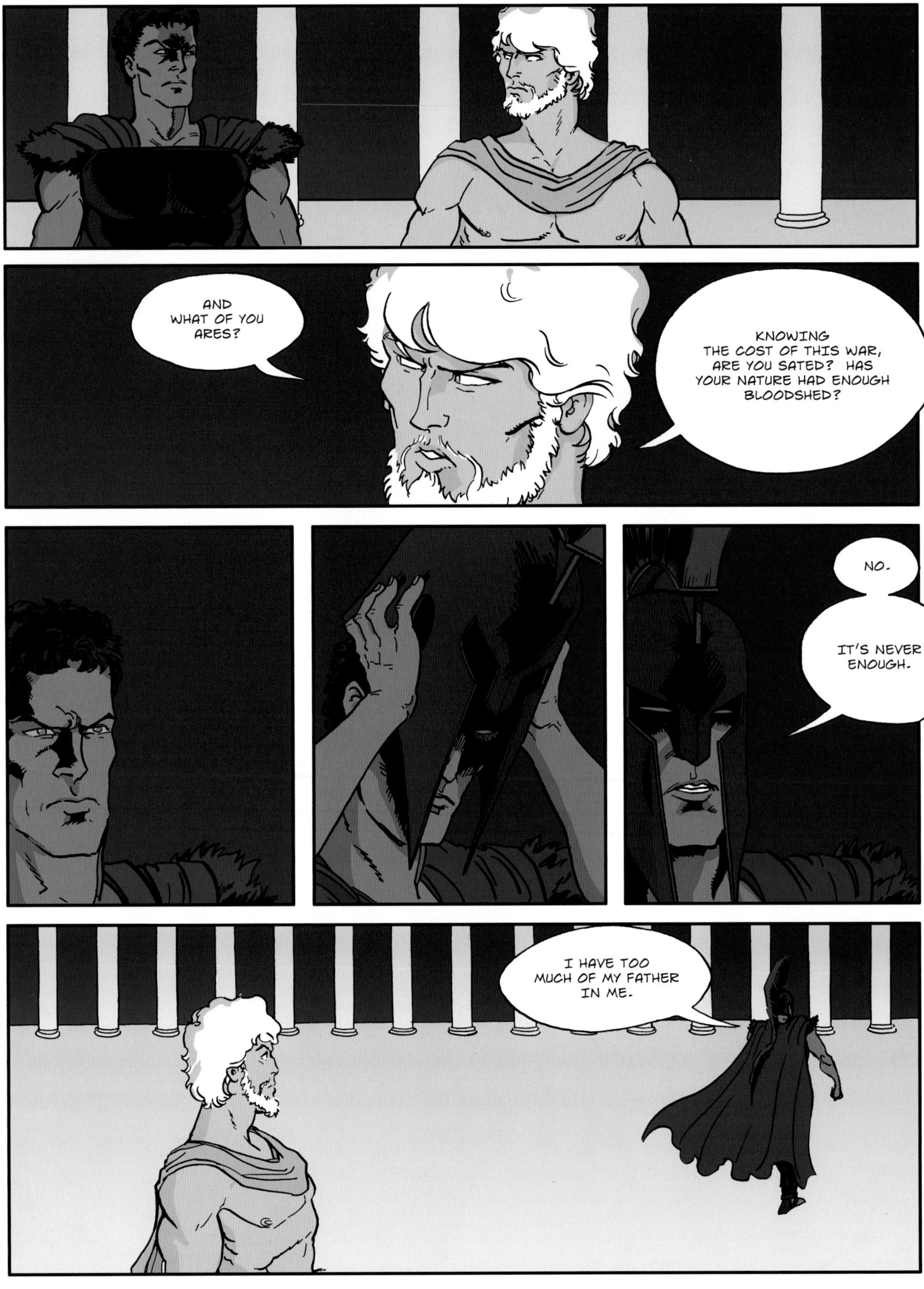
AND WHAT OF YOU ARES?
KNOWING THE COST OF THIS WAR, ARE YOU SATED? HAS YOUR NATURE HAD ENOUGH BLOODSHED?
NO.
IT'S NEVER ENOUGH.
I HAVE TOO MUCH OF MY FATHER IN ME.

AUTHOR'S NOTE

I've met a lot of Athenas in my day.

I've also met a handful of Aphrodites, a few Hermeses, and an Apollo and an Artemis or two. Both a Heracles and a Hera. I even met a Zeus, a young guy maybe ten years old.

I make a lot of appearances, at schools, bookstores, and the like, and it's always exciting to meet mythologically named fans. Honestly, I'm a little envious of someone who gets to go through life as a Dionysus or a Persephone. But there is one godly name that I've encountered more than any other—almost as much as every other name combined. Can you guess who?

If you guessed Ares, congratulations (although really, since you're holding his book, it shouldn't be that much of a surprise). Now to be fair, a good number of these Areses whom I've met are actually Aristides, but since that name means "son of Ares" I still count it. Why are so many people naming their baby sons Ares? Don't they know who Ares is? He's described by words like bloodthirsty, violent, man-slaughtering, murderous—words I rarely hear being used to describe a baby. Even his own father didn't like Ares!

When the time came to tell the story of Ares in OLYMPIANS, I thought this would be a good chance to tell the story of the *Iliad*. The *Iliad* is the first of two ancient epic poems attributed to the Greek poet Homer. It's set during the famous Trojan War, and is largely concerned with the Greek demigod Achilles and his wrathful anger. The Olympians appear throughout, watching and scheming from afar, but also getting down and dirty in the proceedings.

With a focus on the gods' role in the Trojan War it only made sense that Ares should step to the fore. One of the themes of the book is a comparison and contrast between Ares and Athena, the other Grecian war deity. Another significant theme that presented itself was the relationship of Ares to his father, Zeus (not good), and Ares himself as a father. A lot of semi-divine offspring meet their end in the *Iliad*, and the only god we see mourn their child is Ares. Violent Ares, bloodthirsty Ares, most-hated-god-on-Olympus Ares . . . is also sensitive father Ares.

Hmm, maybe that's why so many people name their children Aristides.

George O'Connor
Brooklyn, NY
2014

Adapting a very famous epic poem that is 15,693 lines into a sixty-six-page page graphic novel may sound like a job for a lunatic, but . . . well, yeah, I have no comeback for that. In order to make this work, I had to limit the scope of what I showed. For some reason, there have been quite a few retellings of the Iliad that completely omit the gods—Wolfgang Petersen's 2004 movie *Troy*, for example, or Eric Shanower's excellent ongoing comics series *Age of Bronze*—but for me, the godly bits are the most exciting part.

ARES
GOD OF WAR

GOD OF	War (the destructive, frenzied side of it)
ROMAN NAME	Mars
SYMBOLS	Spear, Helmet, Sword
SACRED ANIMALS	Woodpecker, Vulture, Dog, Rooster
SACRED PLACES	Thrace (site of his birth and center of his cult), Sparta (most warlike of the Greek nations), the Areopagus ("rock of Ares," a hill in Athens where criminal trials were held)
DAY OF THE WEEK	Tuesday
MONTH	March
HEAVENLY BODY	The planet Mars
MODERN LEGACY	The rockets designed to carry the next generation of space vehicles into orbit are called Ares, after the god. The word "martial," as in martial arts, is derived from Ares's Roman name, Mars. It means, appropriately, "warlike." ♂, the gender symbol for men, is a representation of Ares's spear and shield.

G^REEK NOTES

PAGES 4–5: Intro our hero. This was a fun spread to draw, and that's no lie.

PAGE 6 PANEL 1: Speaking of fun, I was super excited to get a chance to draw Eris, goddess of troublemaking again—she ended up being my favorite part of the previous volume of OLYMPIANS, *Aphrodite: Goddess of Love*. I was so enamored of the character of Eris that in the early stages of *Ares* I spent a while trying to install her as narrator. That was a bad idea because (a) she hardly appears in the *Iliad*, the epic poem by Homer that provides the framework for this book, and (b) since she's crazier than an outhouse rat she makes for a spectacularly unreliable narrator.

PAGE 6 PANEL 4: Deimos and Phobos are more personified abstracts concepts than actual gods, hence their spooky wraithlike appearances.

PAGE 8 PANEL 4: At multiple times in the *Iliad*, Ares is referred to as "blood-dripping," as if he's always coated in other people's blood. Pretty gross.

PAGE 9 PANEL 2: Ares's son Askalaphos is not the same dude as Askalaphos the gardener of Hades, whom we met on page 51 of *Hades: Lord of the Dead*. I guess in ancient Greece "owl" was a pretty popular name. Also note he calls himself Greek—strictly speaking that's inaccurate. The *Iliad* predates the word Greek. They would have called themselves either Achaians or Danaans. I just used Greek because it's more familiar to our ears.

PAGE 10: It may seem like I'm dropping you in the middle of the action, but this is pretty much exactly where the *Iliad* begins. People tend to think of it as the story of the Trojan War, but it really covers only a few weeks in the war's tenth year, and doesn't even go to the end.

PAGE 11: Iris, in addition to being the goddess of the rainbow, is the messenger of the gods when Hermes is busy. Considering all the stuff that guy has to do I'm surprised we don't see more of her.

PAGES 12–13 PANEL 1: Here we see the assembled dramatis personae of Mount Olympus for this story—a different assemblage than we normally see in most myths. From left to right, we have Ares, Iris, Aphrodite, Poseidon, Leto, Apollo, Artemis, Hephaistos, Athena, Hera, Hermes, Zeus, and Thetis. The addition of Thetis makes sense, as her son Achilles is the crux of so much of the story of the *Iliad*. Leto, mother of Artemis and Apollo, is a more curious addition to the proceedings, especially given her longstanding enmity with Hera (as seen very briefly in OLYMPIANS Book 3, *Hera: The Goddess and Her Glory*). Noticeably absent are Demeter, Hestia, and Dionysos, though all three are mentioned in the *Iliad*. Hades, not a true Olympian, makes his unseen presence felt elsewhere in the story.

PAGE 14 PANELS 1 AND 2: Flashback courtesy of OLYMPIANS Book 6, *Aphrodite: Goddess of Love*.

PAGE 15 PANEL 3: That's Priam, king of Troy, and Helen, the most beautiful woman in the world watching from the ramparts.

PAGE 20: Remember what I said a few comments ago about how Hades makes his unseen presence felt elsewhere? Get it? It's his helmet of invisibility! SEE HOW FUNNY I AM? Hermes, of course, is dispatched to get it because he's the only Olympian who can freely enter the Underworld. Athena needs it because the helmet makes its wearer invisible, even to other gods.

PAGE 22 PANELS 1–3: Cameos by a few of the greatest heroes of the Trojan War. High King Agamemnon (who we first met a few pages ago), Ajax, the strongest of the Greeks (who is best known today for lending his name to the scouring cleanser), and Odysseus, eponymous star of the *Odyssey* and whom we first met in OLYMPIANS Book 5, *Poseidon: Earth Shaker*.

PAGE 25: Diomedes, the King of Argos, is not to be confused with the Diomedes of Thrace, who was fed to his own man-eating horses by Heracles on page 45 of OLYMPIANS Book 3, *Hera: The Goddess and Her Glory*. Apparently Diomedes and Askalaphos were the Michael and Jacob of their day.

PAGE 27 PANEL 1: Elysium being the paradise where you went after you died if you were "lucky" enough to die valiantly in battle.

PAGE 28 PANEL 6: Apollo is an oracular god, so he would know. After the fall of Troy, Aeneas goes on to found what will eventually become Rome. That's a pretty important fate, I suppose.

PAGE 31 PANEL 1: Intro of Prince Hektor, older brother of Paris and next in line for the throne of Troy after Priam. Hektor is a pretty fascinating character, being arguably the most noble and sympathetic character in the *Iliad*, and he's a Trojan, ostensibly the bad guys.

PAGE 32 PANEL 1: The *Iliad* describes how Ares is everywhere among the Trojans, and how "he ranged now in front of Hektor, and now behind him" in the "likeness of a man mortal." I chose to depict this as multiple, um, Areses, swarming all over the Greek battlements. We are seeing this scene from Diomedes's enchanted eyes, but to the average participant it would look like a crowd of ordinary Trojans. Whether Ares had split himself into multiple incarnations or whether he was moving so fast as to appear in several places at once I leave to you, the reader, to decide.

PAGE 33: The word *stentorian*, an adjective describing a person's voice as "loud and powerful," enters our vernacular from Hera's impersonation here.

PAGE 33 PANEL 9: The *Iliad* specifically mentions that the oaken axle of the chariot groans in protest when Athena steps on it. It's a cool little detail, that gods weigh more than mortals, that my geeky, growing-up-reading-the-official-handbook-of-the-Marvel-Universe self loves.

PAGE 36 PANEL 3: One of my favorite lines from the *Iliad*. To quote Lattimore's translation: "Then Ares the brazen bellowed with a sound as great as nine thousand men make, or ten thousand."

PAGE 37 PANEL 2: Previous recordholder was Heracles, who in various tellings wounded various Olympians, but never two in one day. Take that, Heracles!

PAGE 38: Even though he's known as blood-dripping Ares, that gold stuff isn't blood. The immortal Olympians had a substance called ichor coursing through their veins.

PAGE 41 PANEL 5: It says a lot about Ares that even though his son was Greek, and was killed by a Trojan, that he's going to exact revenge on the Greeks.

PAGE 43 PANEL 1: The composition of this panel is an homage to one of my favorite paintings *Jupiter and Thetis*, by Jean Auguste Dominique Ingres. Check it out—Jupiter (Zeus) couldn't look more diesel. The incident with the hekatoncheires can be seen in OLYMPIANS Book 5, *Poseidon: Earth Shaker*.

PAGE 44 PANEL 4: And this is a tale for another day.

PAGE 46: In some later stories, Thetis made Achilles invincible by dipping him in the River Styx. His only vulnerable spot was his heel, which was where she held him as she dunked him. In Homer's *Iliad*, no mention is made of this supposed invincibility—in fact, in Book 21, an ambidextrous Trojan named Asteropaios throws two spears at him at once and actually draws blood on Achilles' arm. I figure though, any demigod wearing a set of custom armor forged by Hephaistos himself is gonna be plenty hard enough to kill even without being absolutely invincible.

PAGE 46: Achilles is the king of the Myrmidons, a legendary group of people whose name meant "ant-people." To that effect I based elements of his Hephaistos-designed armor on ants.

PAGE 50: Moral of the story is: don't mestus with Hephaistos.

PAGE 52–53: GOD ON GOD ACTION! CAN YOU FEEL THE EXCITEMENT? This sequence is the mythological equivalent of when the Avengers bump into the X-Men. They're both on the same side, but you know when they meet that there'll be a misunderstanding or something that will result in Thor punching Wolverine into orbit or some other similarly awesome event.

PAGE 58 PANEL 5: I'm pretty sure that this is the only punch that's been thrown in the whole series.

PAGE 61: Achilles's mistreatment of the body of Hektor was a huge cultural no-no and was a big part of the reason the gods were so upset with the Greeks after the war.

PAGE 63–64: Contrary to popular belief, The Iliad does not conclude with the end of the Trojan War, but rather with the funeral of Hektor after Hermes is successful in aiding Priam at reclaiming his son's body from Achilles. Provided for your edification, here are the descriptions of the remaining beats of the war depicted in the illustrations.

PAGE 63 PANEL 2: The death of the Amazon Queen Penthesilea, a Trojan ally and the daughter of Ares, at the hands of Achilles.

PAGE 63 PANEL 4: Achilles meets his end from an arrow in the heel fired by Paris, the source of the expression Achilles heel.

PAGE 64 PANEL 1: The Trojan horse. The Greeks pretended to retreat, and presented to the Trojans a giant wooden horse as a sort of goodbye gift. In actuality, it was secretly filled with Greek soldiers. After it was brought into Troy, they snuck out at night and sacked and burned the city. Source of the expression "Trojan horse" and "beware of Greeks bearing gifts," it was seen briefly before in OLYMPIANS Book 5, *Poseidon: Earth Shaker*. Cassandra, sister of Hektor and Paris who was gifted with the power of prophecy and cursed that no one would believe her, begs futilely for the horse not to be brought into Troy.

PAGE 64 PANEL 3: The sack of Troy. In the foreground, King Priam is being clubbed to death by Neoptolemos, the son of Achilles. In the background, in what is surely the most disturbing incident in all of Greek mythology, Greek soldiers throw Hektor's infant son Astyanax off the walls of Troy.

PAGE 64 PANEL 5: Aeneas escapes Troy, with his father, son, and the Palladium, a wooden statue of Athena that was meant to protect the city. As already noted, Aeneas founds what will eventually become Rome in Italy. His story is told in the Roman epic poem the *Aeneid*. The Palladium remained for years in Rome, housed in the temple of Vesta. Supposedly it was transferred out of Rome to Constantinople by Constantine and is now lost.

PAGE 66 PANEL 6: Zing! And that's the end of another installment of G(r)eek Notes. See you all next time.

ABOUT THIS BOOK

ARES: BRINGER OF WAR is the seventh book in OLYMPIANS, a graphic novel series from First Second that retells the Greek myths.

FOR DISCUSSION

1 Who do you like better, Ares or Athena? Who would you rather meet? Who do you think you are more similar to?

2 Why do you think that Zeus dislikes Ares so much? Was it nice to say those things in front of everybody?

3 The gods get in a big fight with one another in this book. Who are some of the gods that you would like to see fight each other?

4 How many soldiers are in this book? You should totally count them (don't really, you'll go crazy).

5 Where do you think Demeter, Hestia, and Dionysos were during this book?

6 This is the first volume of OLYMPIANS in which that tricky George didn't sneak in the line "Mount Olympus, the tallest mountain left standing." What do you think about that?

7 Ares is arguably the most handsome of the gods, but also arguably the most violent. Why do you think that is?

8 Very few people believe in the Greek gods today. Why do you think it is important that we still learn about them?

ERIS

TROUBLEMAKER OF THE GODS

GODDESS OF	Strife, Discord, Arguments
ALSO KNOWN AS	Enyo
ROMAN NAME	Discordia
SYMBOL	Apple of Discord
HEAVENLY BODY	The dwarf planet Eris
MODERN LEGACY	There is a genus of jumping spiders which, while not poisonous or particularly big, are very bitey and terrifying-looking, and so are appropriately named after Eris.

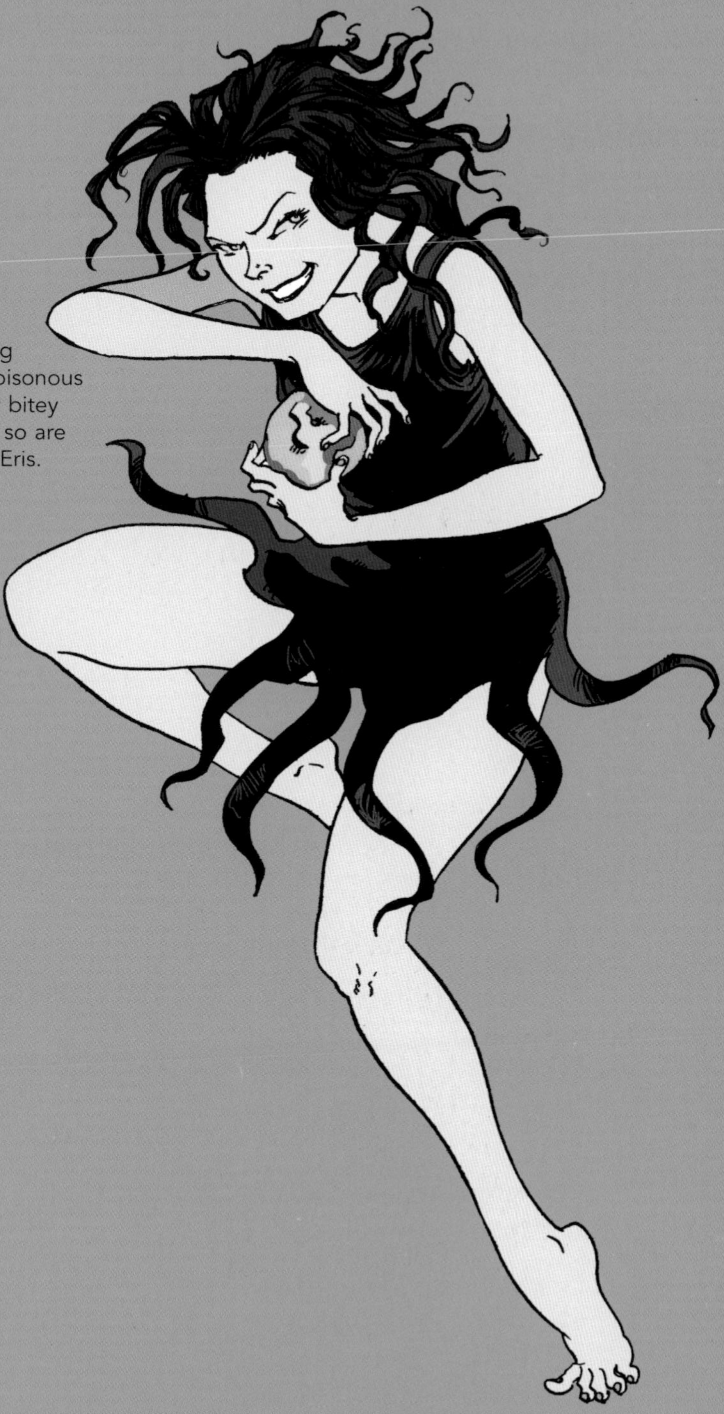

BIBLIOGRAPHY

HOMER. THE ILIAD, TRANSLATED BY RICHMOND LATTIMORE.
UNIVERSITY OF CHICAGO PRESS, 1951.

Ares: Bringer of War is unusual in the OLYMPIANS series because its source material was primarily this single book. There are many translations of the *Iliad* available, but I used this one as it's widely held that Lattimore's does the best job of preserving the flavor of the ancient Greek. Consequently, however, it was a bit of a slog. I had previously read the Robert Fagles version; that one might be said to have a little more pizzazz going on, language-wise.

THEOI GREEK MYTHOLOGY WEB SITE   WWW.THEOI.COM

An online archive of hundreds of ancient Greek and Roman texts. Many of these have never been published in the traditional sense, and many are just fragments recovered from ancient papyrus, or recovered text from other authors' quotations of lost epics. Invaluable.

MYTH INDEX WEB SITE   WWW.MYTHINDEX.COM

Another mythology Web site connected to Theoi.com. While it doesn't have the painstakingly compiled quotations from ancient texts, it does offer some impressive encyclopedic entries on virtually every character to ever pass through a Greek myth. Pretty amazing.

ALSO RECOMMENDED

FOR YOUNGER READERS

D'Aulaires' Book of Greek Myths. Ingri and Edgar Parin D'Aulaire. New York: Doubleday, 1962.

Black Ships Before Troy. Rosemary Sutcliff and Alan Lee. London: Francis Lincoln, 2005.

FOR OLDER READERS

The Marriage of Cadmus and Harmony. Robert Calasso. New York: Knopf, 1993.

Mythology. Edith Hamilton. New York: Grand Central Publishing, 1999.

The Lost Books of the Odyssey. Zachary Mason. New York: Farrar, Strauss and Giroux, 2010.

The Age of Bronze. Graphic novel series. Eric Shanower. Berkley, CA: Image Comics, 2001.

ACHILLES

GREATEST WARRIOR OF THE TROJAN WAR

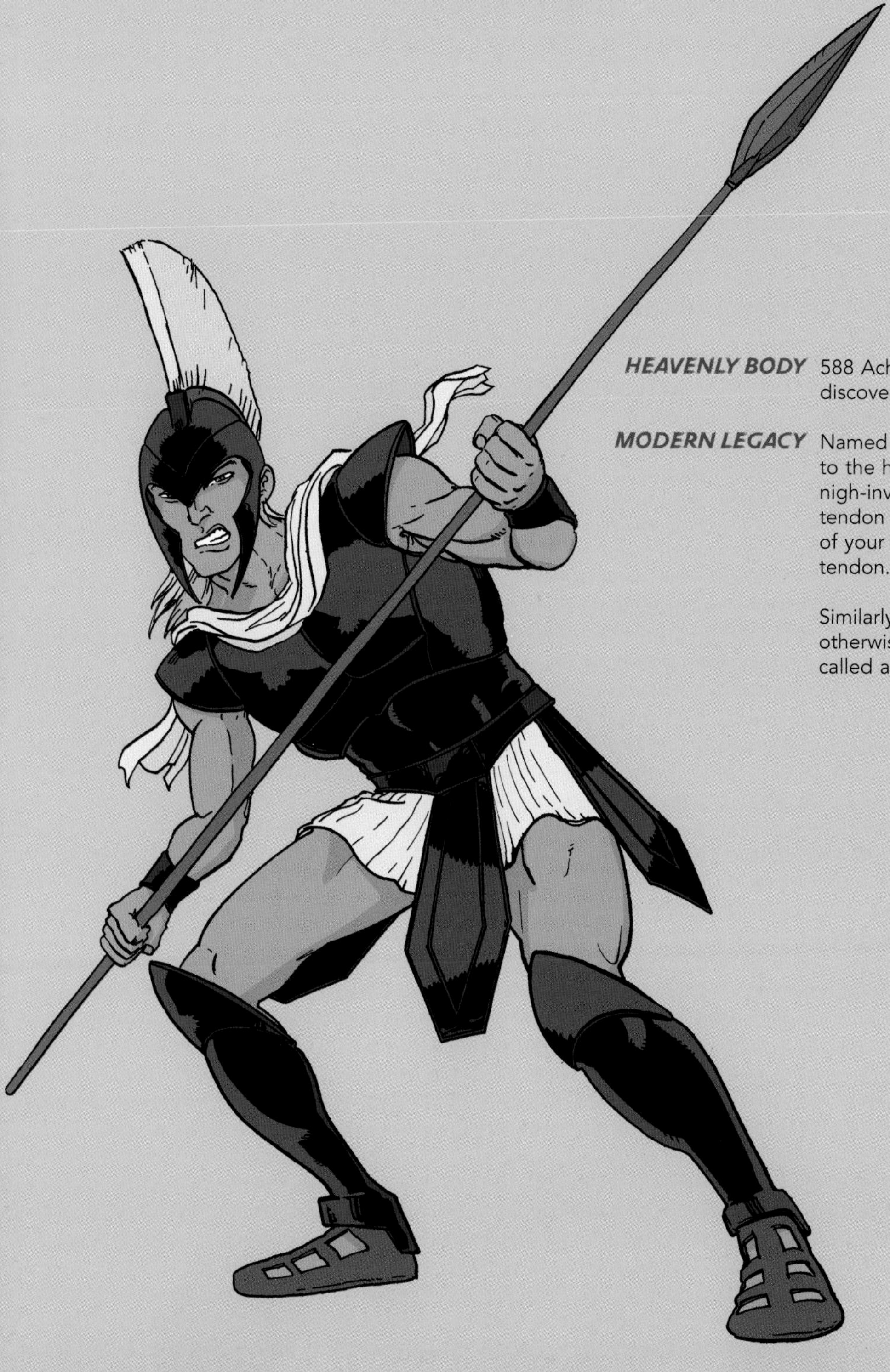

HEAVENLY BODY 588 Achilles, the first asteroid discovered

MODERN LEGACY Named in reference to the injury to the heel that brought down this nigh-invulnerable Greek hero, the tendon that runs down the back of your leg is called the Achilles tendon.

Similarly, any weakness in an otherwise impregnable object is called an Achilles heel.

To all those who have ever fought the good fight

—G.O.

:01
First Second

New York

Copyright © 2015 by George O'Connor

Published by First Second
First Second is an imprint of Roaring Brook Press,
a division of Holtzbrinck Publishing Holdings Limited Partnership
175 Fifth Avenue, New York, New York 10010

Library of Congress Cataloging-in-Publication Data

O'Connor, George.
Ares : bringer of war / George O'Connor. — First edition.
      pages cm. — (Olympians ; 7)
    "A Neal Porter Book."
   Summary: "The myth continues in the tenth year of the fabled Trojan War where two infamous
gods of war go to battle"— Provided by publisher.
   ISBN 978-1-62672-013-8 (paperback)
   ISBN 978-1-62672-014-5 (paper over board)
1. Ares (Greek deity)—Juvenile literature. 2. Trojan War—Juvenile literature. 3. Ares (Greek deity)—Comic
books, strips, etc. 4. Trojan War—Comic books, strips, etc. I. Title.
   BL820.M2O26 2014
   741.5'973—dc23

                          2014041225

First Second books may be purchased for business or promotional use.
For information on bulk purchases please contact Macmillan Corporate
and Premium Sales Department at (800) 221-7945 x5442 or by email at
specialmarkets@macmillan.com.

FIRST
EDITION

First Edition 2015

Cover design by Colleen AF Venable
Book design by Rob Steen

Printed in China by Toppan Leefung Printing Ltd., Dongguan City, Guangdong Province

Paperback: 10 9 8 7 6 5 4
Hardcover: 10 9 8 7 6 5 4 3